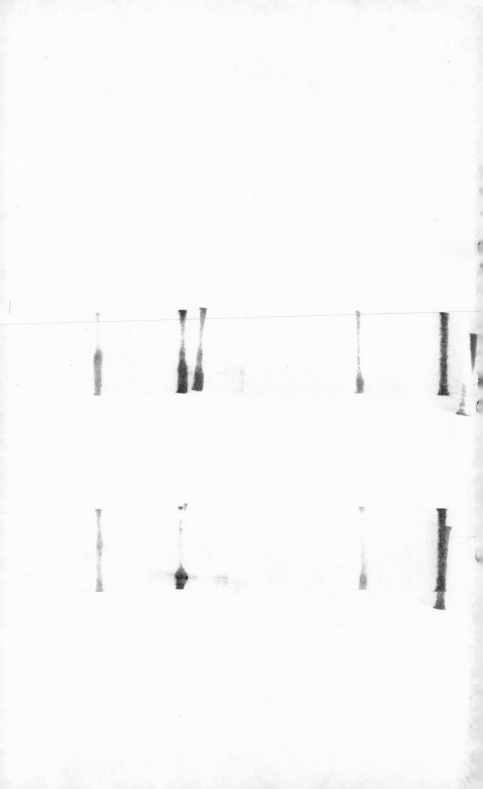

Unseemly End

RODERIC JEFFRIES

Unseemly End

An Inspector Alvarez novel

St. Martin's Press
New York

Unseemly End

CHAPTER 1

Mark Erington heard the vacuum-cleaner switched on in the dining-room and he stood. It would take Victoriana at least ten minutes to clean the floor, after which she'd probably dust down the furniture: ten minutes, anyway, was time enough. He crossed to the French windows and looked beyond the patio to see whereabouts Matas was working in the garden. Matas was leaning on a mattock handle under the shade of an almond tree beyond the wide sweep of lawn and hedge. He smiled. Matas was a rogue, which created a slight bond between them. Matas would idle away the time until the car returned and then he'd start working. No need to fear that he would be prying.

Lulu—a chihuahua, even uglier than the breed standards demanded—plodded from the hall into the sitting-room and collapsed in the middle of the Kirman carpet and panted. Normally, he hated small, snuffly dogs, but he went over, leaned down, and stroked her. She had become his lucky mascot ever since he would have been caught red-handed had she not brought up her lunch of chicken breasts on the pink, blue, and white carnations and roses of the Kirman carpet. Dolly, who'd not been due back for at least another hour but who had that moment stepped into the hall from outside, had shrieked that her beloved was dying and had rushed into the sitting-room where she'd called hysterically for help. He'd managed to creep unseen out of the study and then appear as a ministering angel, shocked but not unnerved by the narrow margin by which he had escaped disaster.

He passed through the arched doorway into the hall. The house possessed a plenitude of archways, both inside and outside, together with a third floor that was one vast open space, and he'd once jokingly compared it to a Persian brothel, but that had been a very bad mistake because Dolly had not been in the least amused. She loved the house, not because of its eccentricities, but because it was the largest within several kilometres of Llueso.

Two paintings hung on opposite walls in the hall. Original Montague Dawsons. A visiting British art dealer had valued them at over a million pesetas each. Regrettably, he'd never been able to find reproductions good enough to substitute for the originals.

The study, with its arched doorway, was on the north side of the hall. It was large and high-ceilinged and it contained as well as much more pedestrian pieces, some furniture of remarkable quality which included two matching mahogany secretaire bookcases whose shelves, behind astragal doors, were filled with leather-bound books whose subjects ranged from the classics to modern biographies and novels. Originally, he'd believed these were kept merely to create an impression, but then he'd learned that Dolly had read all of them and could discuss any of them with intelligence and he'd immediately revised his opinion of her: she was not nearly as stupid as her manner normally suggested.

The kneehole desk, attributed to Thomas Hardy the Elder, in walnut and yew, had one long drawer and then, on either side of the kneehole, three narrow drawers of unequal depths. The long drawer and the top left-hand narrow drawer were always kept locked. He took from his trouser pocket a skeleton key which looked rather like a double-ended dentist's pick and used one end to force the lock of the long drawer. He pulled the drawer open.

Dolly was as untidy, though not careless, in her financial affairs as she was in all others, but since the letter from the Swiss bank had arrived the previous morning it was on top of the tangled mass of correspondence and papers. He opened the cartridge paper envelope and brought out the letter and folded statement it contained. The letter was subservient in form, yet in tone it was larded with Swiss banking astringency. Herr Strauss was delighted to send to the bank's esteemed client the statement of account which she had requested in her letter of the 18th. Should there be anything more she desired, in particular the purchase of any investments, the bank would be honoured to act to her orders . . . He unfolded the statement, read the final figure, and whistled. When one remembered that she also had accounts in England, Jersey, America, and locally . . . He replaced the letter and statement in the envelope, dropped the envelope back on top of the pile, shut the drawer and relocked it. He unlocked the top left-hand narrow drawer. In this, she kept her reserve of Spanish money—afraid of having her handbag stolen, she never carried in it more than five thousand pesetas in cash. In the drawer was a jumble of five-thousand, one-thousand, and five-hundred-peseta notes. He helped himself to one five-thousand, three one-thousand, and two five-hundred notes. He could have taken more without her suspecting anything, but a wise man knew just how far to go. He relocked the drawer. He stepped out into the hall and the vacuum-cleaner was still working. He smiled with satisfaction. Almost certainly, Victoriana would not have thought anything of seeing him walk out of the study, but no man ever got himself hanged by being too careful.

He walked through the sitting-room, pausing to pat Lulu on her domed head, and out to the covered patio. He stood by one of the chairs and ran his fingers through his tight, curly black hair as he stared out at the garden. Large lawn, which would soon cost a fortune to keep watered in the scorching heat because the well would run dry and the water would have to be bought by the lorry load, flower-beds filled with colour, a centuries

old, gnarled, deformed olive tree which had been trans-
planted three years before, jacaranda, mimosa, and
acacia trees, now all past blooming but still attractive
with their feathery or trailing leaves, hibiscus bushes with
trumpet flowers up to eleven inches in diameter and, to
his left, the very large kidney-shaped swimming pool . . .
Money. Scorned by philosophers, which only showed
what fools wise men could be . . . If there were times when
he knew something approaching self-contempt, he had
only to come and look at the garden to regain his sense of
values.

He went over to the wall of the house and pushed the
bell-push, set next to the telephone extension socket.
Then he sat down, stretched out his legs, and thought
that after he'd had a couple of drinks, he'd have a swim:
and after a swim, he'd have a couple of drinks. He patted
his right-hand trouser pocket. Nine thousand pesetas. He
could take Carol to any of the restaurants in the Port and
come away with change, even if she ordered lobster: not
that she was the kind of person to do that. As yet, he
hadn't decided how best to break free of Dolly for the
night, but it shouldn't be too difficult . . .

Victoriana walked out on to the patio.

'I'm dying of thirst,' he said, in his heavily accented but
fluent Spanish. 'Wheel out the drinks, will you, and make
certain there's lots of ice. It's hot enough now to fry an
egg in the shade.'

'My grandfather says it's going to be a really long summer. The well is already very low and it's still only the
middle of June.'

What if the well did dry up earlier than usual? Dolly
would merely need to buy even more water than normal.
With her money, she could afford to buy Niagara Falls.

Victoriana went indoors. When she returned, she was
wheeling a large cocktail cabinet which ran on castors
and she positioned this close to his chair. 'I've filled the

ice bucket. There ought to be enough in there to keep even you cool.' Her sly grin gave her words a double meaning.

'Then it's safe for you to sit down and have a drink with me, isn't it?'

'I wouldn't go that far.'

'How far would you go?'

She tossed her head. 'I've too much work to do to think of sitting down.'

'Come on, relax.'

'Can't. The señora telephoned half an hour ago, when you were out, to say she's having some friends in to dinner. So I've got to do the house and then start getting the grub ready.'

His voice lost its bantering tone: he spoke bad-temperedly. 'D'you mean dinner tonight?'

' 'Course I mean tonight.'

He swore, in English.

'What's that mean?'

'I'm glad.'

She giggled.

'Who's coming?'

'The señora just said it was two people.'

Dolly would never let him go out for the evening now. She'd want him to be there to do all the entertaining if she became bored, to flatter her, to prompt her if she felt like telling one of her stories, to fuss round her . . . Hell, he thought, why bother to go on? Tonight, then, there'd be no dinner à deux with Carol. But Dolly's nine thousand pesetas would still be there for another time . . .

'I suppose I'd better get back to work,' said Victoriana, speaking as if reluctant to do so and forgetting that only a minute before she had said she was in a rush. She waited, but when he made no comment she went into the house.

Mallorquin women, he thought, ripened early, bloomed but briefly, aged prematurely. Victoriana still bloomed. Her features were attractive in a bold, obvious manner, made still more obvious by her use of make-up: her mouth was large, her lips full and moist. Her figure was genuinely shapely. A rose eager to be plucked . . . Yet to mess around with her while living under Dolly's roof would be the act of an idiot: Dolly kept her eyes very wide open.

He stood and pondered what to drink, finally chose a sweet vermouth and soda. And as he poured out the drink, he reflected sadly that it was unfortunate, but true, that in this life one couldn't have everything.

CHAPTER 2

Cynthia Rockford stubbed her toe on a loose stone. 'Blast!'

'What's the matter?' her husband asked.

'I've just hurt my toe because you will insist on shining the torch in the wrong direction.'

'Sorry about that,' he said, with unfailing good humour, as he redirected the torch to point directly in front of her.

'Why on earth couldn't we use the car?'

'It's such a short way . . .'

'It's not very short when I all but break a toe.'

They continued along the dirt track, some four metres wide, which was bordered on one side by weed grass, already parched brown, brambles, and a stone wall a metre high, and on the other by the dip down to the field beyond. Overhead, the sky was cloudless and the stars diamond bright. Rockford looked up and inadvertently altered the aim of the torch.

'Do you think,' she asked, with strained patience, 'that you could manage to concentrate on what you're doing just until we get home?'

'As a matter of fact, old girl, I glanced up and saw Arcturus and remembered the time in the North Sea . . .'

'I know the story off by heart.'

'Really? . . . But it was a bit odd, you know.'

'I've never been able to see the slightest thing odd about it.'

He was not surprised. Cynthia had her feet planted firmly on the ground: the mysteries of life annoyed rather than intrigued her.

They reached their bungalow and turned into the garden. The edge of the torch beam picked out parched earth and a few tired-looking plants and shrubs, chosen for their ability to resist drought. He unlocked the front door, reached in and switched on the light in the very small passage, which was also the hall, then stepped aside. She went in and past the tiny kitchen on the right to the sitting-room beyond, where she switched on all the five lights in the overhead cluster in the centre of the ceiling. He followed her, after shutting the front door, and without thinking about what he was doing switched off three of the lights.

'Can't we now even afford to see what we're doing?' she asked sharply.

He shrugged his broad shoulders and switched the three lights back on again. Unless they were going to read, they didn't need all five lights on, using up quite a lot of electricity, but it was no good trying to reason with her: not after an evening spent at Ca Na Nadana.

She sat in one of the very well worn armchairs. 'That woman is quite impossible.'

'Dolly is a bit of a character,' he said. He noticed that her angular face was set in lines of bitterness. She wore an attractive, hand-embroidered blouse and a long, flared skirt in a warm shade of rust brown, but at the beginning of the evening she had sharply reminded him that the blouse was seven and the skirt five years old . . . It hadn't helped, of course, to find Dolly dressed in a new frock which had obviously cost a great deal of money.

He knew — and was fairly certain that she did not — that among the local expatriates she was often referred to as the Ice Maiden. He didn't think there was a double meaning to the word 'maiden', but if there were, then people were surprisingly well informed about certain details of his married life. She had long since brought an end to 'all that nonsense' . . .

'It was in the worst possible taste to go on and on telling us how her son-in-law is making so much money and what a big house he and Samantha have bought.'

'I suppose she is rather proud of them.'

'Proud of how wealthy they are.'

Since it was difficult to deny that, he didn't try.

'It was appallingly ostentatious to have so much silver on the table.'

'D'you really think so? I rather care for a few bits of silver about the place . . .'

'A few bits of silver! Really, Phillip! That épergne would only not have been out of place in the Guildhall. And it needed a table twice as long to take two of those candelabra, let alone all four. And I never have been able to stand queen's pattern: quite vulgar. The whole thing was done just to impress us.'

He chuckled. 'I was impressed.'

Her mouth tightened a fraction more. 'And it was for precisely the same reason that she served Veuve Clicquot, which costs ten times as much as one of the best Spanish sparkling wines and isn't any better.'

'I thought you always said there wasn't any comparison?'

'I have never said anything of the sort.'

He looked across at the carved wooden chest in which they kept their drinks. A nightcap would be doubly welcome.

'As for that creature, Mark . . . It's an insult to ask us when he's there.'

'But he's there all the time so how can she do anything else?'

'It's quite disgusting for a woman to live with a man half her age.'

'I don't see that. They're happy and they don't disturb anyone else, so where's the harm?'

'I can certainly rely on you to make excuses for that sort of behaviour.'

'Don't forget, old girl, this isn't Cheltenham.'

'What a ridiculous thing to say.'

'What I mean is, on this island things are a bit different. Life's more free and easy than at home.'

'Which is, no doubt, why you insisted on moving out here.'

He walked over to the wooden chest and raised the lid.

'What are you doing, Phillip?'

'Getting us both a nightcap.'

'I don't want one. And you've had quite enough already.'

'D'you remember old Archie? "Enough's enough, but quite enough's not quite enough." Always used to quote that just before he passed out. There was that party in Cape Town . . .'

'He was an alcoholic.'

'Come off it, Cyn! It's just that he liked a good party. You know as well as I do that he never touched the stuff at sea and even went dry the night before sailing so that he'd be on the top line right from the start. I can remember . . .'

'Haven't I suffered enough of your reminiscences for one night?'

He leaned over and reached down for the bottle of Soberano, carried this through to the kitchen. He poured himself out a large tot, added soda and ice, and returned to the sitting-room. He replaced the brandy in the chest: Cynthia did not like to find any bottles left around the place.

'How that woman can go on and on behaving as she does without realizing how ridiculous she makes herself . . . The trouble is, of course, the nouveau riche never has known how to behave.'

He lifted his glass and was about to drink when he suddenly chuckled. 'In her case, it's surely the nouvache riche?'

'What on earth are you talking about?'

'At her age, she's more vache than veau.'

She said, in bitter tones of exasperation: 'For God's sake, try to think of other people for once. Surely even you can understand that I've already had more than enough to put up with tonight?'

He had enjoyed puns ever since he had been young. At the age of twelve, when at a West Country preparatory school, he had, in an exam, translated pas de tout as 'Thy Father'. Despite the fact that it was the end of term the headmaster had administered a beating, not because of the weakness of the pun, when it would have been justified, but because he—a very earnest man—thought he detected blasphemy. During their engagement, Cynthia had persuaded Rockford to forgo so juvenile a vice, but within two years of their marriage he had returned to it. The truth was, though this was never even hinted at, that although he tried so hard in every other respect to accede to her wishes, in the resumption of this vice he allowed himself his one cri de coeur (a dog's appeal) against the unhappier aspects of the marriage which, it had turned out, offered none of the warm tenderness a man of his caring nature needed.

She left the room. He sat and drank. Her expression of disdainful resentment had made her look just like her mother, Lady Hobson. He remembered when he'd joined HMS *Nestor* as a raw, somewhat nervous sub-lieutenant, very conscious that his background was different from most of the other officers—he came from yeoman stock—yet in no way lacking in self-confidence when it came to professional skills. He'd had no private income, and in those days many officers had, and in a priggish way he had been proud of the fact and contemptuous of those who did—until he'd come to appreciate the stupidity of his attitude, he'd made few friends. He had, therefore, been very grateful to be introduced to one of Admiral Sir Hugh Hobson's daughters, who in turn had introduced him to her two sisters. They'd all had fun together—in the old-fashioned sense of the word: games of croquet and tennis, picnics, dances . . . One evening the admiral had called him into the study. 'My boy,' the admiral had said in the booming voice which had earned him his nickname of Force Tenner—a reference to the Beaufort Scale—'as my wife says, you've been seeing a lot of our gals and so must have made up your mind. So which one is it to be for the splicing, eh?' A more sophisticated man might have said that in the face of such dazzling choice it was impossible to choose (look what had befallen Paris), a less dutiful man would have pointed out the impossibility of marrying on a junior officer's pay, but he hadn't been sophisticated and he had believed that an officer and gentleman's responsibility to life lay in his doing his duty, no matter what the cost. This meant that if he had behaved in such a manner as to make it appear to others, and in particular the parents, that he was courting one of the three daughters then plainly it was his duty to accept the consequences of his actions even though these had been misinterpreted. Yet which one to name? . . . Admiral Sir Hugh Hobson had pressed home his advantage with the ruthlessness of a professional strategician. 'It seems to me, my boy, that you're really fond of our gal Cynthia . . .'

He finished the brandy. A classic example of Hobson's choice.

*

'Perhaps I will just have one more little drinkie,' said Dolly.

Erington crossed to the cocktail cabinet, which had been wheeled into the sitting-room. 'Cognac?'

'Only a very small one.'

He poured out a very large measure of Rémy Martin VSOP and crossed the Kirman carpet to hand her the glass. Lulu, who sat on her lap, looked up and snuffled.

'She wants walkies,' Dolly said.

'She can't do. She went out only five minutes ago . . .'

She spoke in her little girl's voice. 'Won't the nasty man give little Lulu walkies?'

He sighed. He picked Lulu off Dolly's lap and put her down on the floor and she followed him out into the hall. He opened the front door.

Dolly called out: 'Do see that that horrid, nasty pi-dog isn't around again to bother Lulu.'

He went outside and closed the door behind himself. 'Find him and have fun,' he said, as Lulu waddled away.

The air was heady with the cloying scent of a lady-of-the-night bush in flower. Cicadas shrilled. Several sheep in one of the nearby fields were moving around and there was a continual noise from the bells they wore round their necks. A scops owl called several times, with the music that the sheep bells lacked. Then, harsh and intrusive, from the direction of the urbanizacion on the lower slopes of the nearest mountain, came the snarling crackle of a powerful car's exhaust. The Ferrari Boxer he'd seen the other day? he wondered enviously.

When he returned to the sitting-room, Dolly had stretched out on the settee, her frock carelessly ruckled about her. It was amazing, he thought, how skilful cosseting and corseting could roll back the years. Among the papers in her desk there had been one in which she had given her age as 50. Knowing her, he added another

5 years. But when she coyly admitted to being 45 she did
not provoke immediate and scornful disbelief. Her round
face was almost unlined and her complexion was the
traditional English peaches-and-cream: her cheeks were
smooth and full without being plump: her golden-brown
hair, either by the gift of nature or the art of the hairdresser, was untinged with grey: her teeth were white and
all her own: her neck showed no hint of the sinewy scrag-
giness which often bedevilled a woman in middle age: her
body, when expertly supported, was maturely shapely:
her ankles could have been those of a twenty-year-old.

'I'm feeling very, very tired,' she said.

'You must be. You always work so very hard to enter-
tain people.' He sometimes amazed himself by his ability
to sound as if he really meant what he said.

'I do work hard. Even when I know it's a waste of time.'

She had begun to sound querulous. Thinking he knew
what had upset her, he said: 'Cynthia can be a difficult
woman.'

Lulu, who had been snuffling her way round the room,
reached the settee. Unable to jump up, she began to
whine. 'She is an exceedingly difficult woman,' Dolly
said, as she reached down to help Lulu up.

He sat. If she wanted to criticize Cynthia, then he'd
join in with enthusiasm. 'She puts on such airs and graces,
but look at that shack she lives in! And when could they
last afford a new car? Retired officers' wives always
behave as if they've the right to sit on the left side of God.'

'She can't talk about anything but the fact that her
father was something or other in the Navy.'

Cynthia would never have been asked to Ca Na
Nadana if her father had not been a knight and an
admiral. 'I thought she was very rude to you.'

'Why shouldn't I tell her how well Samantha's husband
is doing and how they've bought a lovely house in Rich-
mond which may have been rather expensive but has such

a wonderful view over the common?'

'No reason whatsoever, of course.' He laughed to himself. It was impossible, when one knew as much as he did, not to admire the depth of her hypocrisy: and also not to be amazed that any woman could in character be such a mixture of hard cleverness and weak stupidity. She had had the ruthlessness to use her money to secure her social position within the community, yet was weak and stupid enough not to realize that nothing could now deprive her of that position because the wealthy made their own rules. What if her daughter had married a nobody who wasn't a success? Why be so bourgeois as to see this as a disgrace and so invent a very successful son-in-law who bought his beloved wife a munificent house . . . ?

He'd been just as much taken in as anyone else by all the talk of Samantha and her clever husband until he'd broken into Dolly's desk for the first time and come across a long letter from Samantha, written on the cheapest paper, in an envelope addressed to Dolly's bank in London, who had forwarded it. The letter had made it clear that Samantha had rebelled against the artificiality of her mother's life and had deliberately chosen to marry someone of no background: the kind of defiant statement on life which the young found so romantically satisfying, but which so often turned sour. It had turned very sour for Samantha. Her husband had been made redundant by the factory in which he'd worked and he'd had to go on the dole. Money had become so tight they'd had to appeal for supplementary benefits. She'd suffered from bad varicose veins for some time but under the national health would have to wait for ages before an operation: if only she could afford to be a private patient the operation could be done immediately. Her husband, even though they were so desperately short of money, was drinking heavily . . . The list of troubles had been almost endless: a fitting epitaph on idealism. Then had come the punch lines. Could Mummy let bygones be bygones? Couldn't they both make a fresh start and forget all the nasty things which had been said? Couldn't Mummy give her some money to let her have the operation, to help her husband regain his self-respect . . . Attached to the letter by a paper-clip had been a draft answer in Dolly's handwriting: as an accurate commentary on Dolly's character, it could not have been bettered. Inflation was making life difficult for everyone, especially herself, and she was finding it almost impossible to make both ends meet. And had she not repeatedly warned Samantha against the dangers of marrying a man from so different — and undesirable — a background, yet Samantha had ignored the warnings. Once one was an adult, one had to learn to lie on the bed of one's own making . . .

Dolly spoke spitefully to interrupt his memories. 'The trouble with Cynthia is that she's jealous of me with this lovely house and all the lovely things in it.'

'Of which the loveliest is you, darling. You make her look like a dried-up algarroba bean.'

She did not simper with pleasure. She was, he thought, becoming thoroughly bad-tempered and when that happened there was always the possibility that the hard, mean streak in her character, which normally lay well hidden, would come to the surface. Something was worrying her which had not yet come out in the open and instinct warned him that that something was connected with him. He must try to head off the trouble. He smiled at her, knowing how much she loved his smile, and said: 'Let's have another little drinkie and forget the Ice Maiden.' He stood.

'She told me something about you.'

'Then it wasn't at all nice!' He laughed as he crossed, seemingly unhurriedly but in fact as fast as he dared, to the cocktail cabinet where he picked up the bottle of cognac. One could usually divert her attention with drink. He returned to the settee. 'Just a little top up . . .'

'She saw you. You didn't know that, did you?'

His handsome, if weak, face expressed only mild amusement. 'I'm surprised she condescended to remember the fact.'

'You were in the square.'

He filled her glass to within a couple of inches of the brim, conscious that she was angrily watching his face. 'I suppose the real trouble is that I forgot to touch my fore-lock.' He bowed his head, raised his left hand to his forehead, and said with a thick accent: 'Roight 'onoured, yer ledyship, to 'ave the privilege of bein' noticed by 'ee . . .'

'Don't be such a bloody fool. You failed to see her because you were so busy.'

He straightened up as he belatedly realized what the trouble was. He became all solemn and very concerned. 'Dolly, my angel, something seems to be upsetting you. Tell Markie what the trouble is.'

'You met a girl in the square.'

He frowned. 'I'm always meeting people in the square—it's one of the perils of going into the village. But was this someone in particular?'

'Cynthia said she was . . . was very attractive.'

'A very attractive girl I've recently met in the square . . . Do you know, I believe she must mean Carol! And you're telling me she became all bitchily excited over Carol?'

'Who is she?'

'Beyond the fact that Tom introduced me and her sur-name's something like Whitby, I can't answer you.'

'You were having drinks with her.'

'Not plural, singular. One drink.'

'Why?'

'Why what?'

'Why were you drinking with her?'

'Why not?' He shrugged his shoulders. 'When one meets someone like that . . . And she seemed a bit lonely, so I felt sorry for her.'

'Cynthia said she was beautiful.'

'Carol would be flattered. But don't forget that Cynthia judges everyone by herself so that beauty comes easily to the eye of the beholder.'

Some of Dolly's anger lifted. He knelt by the settee, put the bottle down on the floor, and began to stroke her cheek. 'Shall I tell Dolly something? I believe she was becoming just a teeny-weeny bit jealous.'

She pouted. 'From the way Cynthia was talking, I thought this girl must be . . .'

He put his forefinger across her mouth. 'And can you really believe that even if she looked like Venus rising out of the sea in her scallop shell, Markie would be in the slightest bit interested when he's got his Dolly?'

She simpered.

'What a silly girl Dolly can become when a nasty old woman talks a lot of nonsense.' He kissed her cheek. He whispered: 'Markie loves Dolly and only Dolly.' Old bitch, he thought, meaning Cynthia. But at least she'd inadvertently taught him that he'd been all kinds of a fool to think of taking Carol out to a meal.

CHAPTER 3

Carol Whitby was five feet seven tall, in her bare feet. She had naturally curly, blonde hair which she sometimes bothered to have styled and sometimes didn't. Her face was oval, with high cheekbones, her eyes were deep blue, her nose only just missed being turned-up, and her mouth seemed always ready to break into a grin. She had a fashionably slim body and wore very casual clothes most of the time. Three years before she had lived with her parents in south Canterbury, in an undistinguished but pleasant detached house set in a large garden. It was a happy home in which the two generations got on very well together: and when her wishes did not coincide with theirs, she had had little hesitation in playing on their love to get her own way. This was how happy families had always been.

Returning from a holiday in Corfu, she had learned for the first time that her mother had been suffering from considerable pain and discomfort and that a specialist had advised an exploratory operation. It had shocked her, but she had been convinced that although tragedy came to other families, it could not come to hers. The day after the operation, she learned how wrong she'd been: her mother had cancer of the cervix and it was considered inoperable.

Had she ever been asked beforehand what her father's reactions would be to such a situation, she would have said without hesitation that he would be totally distraught yet, with high courage, he would overcome his own feelings in order to support his wife's. Reality was so different that it stunned her. He rejected his wife as if she had suddenly become a stranger: where she needed all possible love and understanding to help her come to terms with the future, she received from him only resentment, as if her terminal illness was entirely of her own making.

Bewildered, sick at heart, bitterly furious, Carol had said all the hurtful things in her mind. He had made no reply: had not once tried to defend himself: by his silence, he had stood condemned.

Her mother, mercifully, had died quite suddenly. At the funeral her father had been very composed. So composed that she had hysterically accused him of never having loved her mother and of even being glad she'd died . . .

He'd committed suicide five weeks later, on the day that would have been their twenty-fifth wedding anniversary. He left two letters, one to the police making it clear he had taken his own life, one to her in which he told her some of the things he had not been able to say. And from this letter she had learned how dreadfully wrong she'd been. He'd treated his wife as he had, not because he'd ceased to love her the moment he'd discovered her life was forfeit, but because, faced by the coming loss, his love had become so overwhelming that the only way in which he could live with it had been for his mind to shut itself off from it.

For a time she'd tortured herself with memories of all she'd thought and said: told herself that if only she'd been more understanding perhaps he would not have committed suicide. But then she came to realize that his letter had made it clear that he'd always realized it was love, not hate, which had provoked her and that nothing could or would have turned him away from suicide.

The double tragedy—triple, if one included her own—had taught her that it was always difficult, perhaps impossible, to judge another human being. She did not try to judge again: she just accepted, careless of convention or sentiment. And this readiness to accept, without question, without judgement, gave her an air of calm goodness—which owed nothing to do-gooding—which was impossible to miss. Luckily for her, since little arouses such antagonism as obvious goodness, she also had a strong sense of humour.

She said, 'I'm hungry.'

George Trent looked down the road towards the bay beyond, a small segment of which was just visible: the water was dead calm and the sky immediately above the crest of the mountain was tinged with the violet of coming dusk.

'In fact,' she continued, 'I'm ravenous because all I had

for lunch was one banana, one apple, and a small yoghurt.'

'You can be on the point of starvation, but I'm not taking you out to a meal.'

'Because you've better things to do?'

'Because I bloody well can't afford to,' he answered angrily. He rubbed his square chin with an oil-stained hand. He had a strongly featured face, almost belligerent-looking about the mouth.

'Well, I can, because I found a thousand-peseta note on the pavement outside the supermarket this morning.'

'You make a lousy liar.'

'It's the truth.'

'For God's sake, Carol! If you had found a thousand-peseta note, the first thing you'd have done would have been to hand it in to one of the cashiers.'

She laughed, because that was true.

He leaned against the car which was parked in the road, immediately outside the garage. 'Look, if I'd got the money I'd take you out to the best meal the Port can offer. But the old bastard who runs the place owes me last week's wages and right now I'm skint.'

'Why hasn't he paid you yet?'

'Because his main pleasure in life is avoiding paying what he owes.'

'Knowing you, I'd have thought you'd have found a way to make him.'

'I have to keep a low profile because I haven't a work permit. The authorities would drop on me like a ton of bricks if they discovered I'd been working here. He knows I can't start shouting, so he has fun not paying me.'

'He wouldn't dare report you or he'd be in just as much trouble for employing you.'

He shook his head. 'He's rich and he knows all the right people: that sort of person never gets into trouble.'

'That's being cynical.'

'Realistic.'

'Then if it really is like that, appeal to his tender feelings.'

'There's no point in appealing to something which doesn't exist.'

A man, dressed only in shorts and sandals, his back and chest lobster red, hurried along the road. He stopped by the car and looked, with a very worried expression, at the closed main doors of the garage.

'Mr Simonds?' asked Trent.

A look of relief came over the man's face. 'Blimey, you speak English! I was getting worried you'd be closed. Sorry I'm a bit after the time said, but we were on the beach and the kids made some friends and time just slipped by . . .'

Trent cut short what could have been a long story. 'Will you come in and sign the papers and then everything's OK. The tank's filled with petrol and I'll be charging for that. We'll give you credit for however much petrol's in the tank when you get back here.'

'I see . . . I say, it is right, isn't it, that picking the car up this late means I'm not charged anything for today?'

'Yes.'

'Just wanted to make certain. I mean, with prices what they are and a family, one has to budget very carefully, you know.'

Trent said to Carol: 'Sorry I can't make it. Be seeing you around.' He led the way through the small doorway, to the side of the main garage doors, and into the office.

Five minutes later, the two men returned. Trent locked the small door, then showed the other the controls of the Seat 133. The man drove off, very carefully keeping to the right.

Carol, who had been looking in the windows of a newsagent and stationer further up the road, walked back along the pavement. 'Don't forget to add half an hour's overtime to your wages this week.'

'And give the boss all the pleasure of refusing to pay it?'

'You obviously need a drink to cheer you up.'

'I've one can of beer left and I'm going back now to my room to drink it.'

'How awful if you'd happened to have had two! . . . George, will you tell me something?'

He took a packet of Celtas cigarettes from his pocket and offered it: she shook her head.

'You took me out to a meal last week and paid for both of us: so why won't you let me take you out this week? Isn't that what women's lib is all about?'

'I thought it was bra burning.'

'Of course . . . Come on, what's wrong with fair shares?'

'I'm not letting any woman pay for me.'

'Why not? And why get so vehement about it?'

He looked at his watch.

'All right, when it comes to stubbornness, compared to you a mule is just a beginner . . . What's sauce for the goose is sauce for the gander, right?'

'What are you getting at?' he asked suspiciously.

'Just that I'm as entitled to principles as you are. I'm not going to have you paying for me. I agree, that's thoroughly immoral. So I owe you four hundred and seventy-five pesetas.'

'You what?'

She was wearing a T-shirt and jeans. She brought a small purse from the right-hand pocket of the jeans, opened it, and produced a five-hundred-peseta note. 'I want twenty-five pesetas change, please.'

'What the hell are you on about?'

'You paid for both of us at the restaurant last week and the bill was nine hundred and fifty pesetas, with the tip: I know because I peeked. So I'm paying you the half I owe you. And now that you're in funds, let's go out and have a meal, Dutch women's lib style.'

'You're not . . .'

'If you argue any further, I'll hit you with a torque converter.'

'You wouldn't know one if you saw it.'

'That's immaterial. Anything heavy enough to hammer the message through your thick skull will do.'

He finally grinned.

'Thank goodness for that! I was beginning to think you were doing a Henry I.'

'What's that supposed to signify?'

'He never smiled again . . . Come on, let's get moving. If I don't soon have something to eat, I'll collapse.'

They walked along the road, away from the direction of the bay. She wondered what had caused him to be so sharp and bitter when she had suggested paying for the meal?

For a long time, Rockford had expected to reach the top of his profession and retire an admiral. A naturally modest man, he was yet able to evaluate his own capabilities and to recognize that he possessed not only the ability to command but also that extra something, that resolution ruthlessly to identify and accept the truth through a fog of wishful thinking, which fitted a man to command from high places. But eventually he had had to accept that he would not rise to flag rank.

After the war the Navy had become in many ways more democratic, but one thing had not changed since pre-war days because it could not be legislated against—the way in which an officer's career could be affected by the behaviour of his wife. Cynthia had never been able to forget that she was the daughter of Admiral Sir Hugh and Lady Hobson. In her eyes this entitled her to say exactly what she thought to whomsoever she wished: also, it placed her in an unassailably high social position. This combination of rudeness and snobbery irritated far more wives of senior officers than it amused and their irritation was made apparent to their husbands. Eventually, a vice admiral, who liked and admired Rockford, took him on one side and said very tactfully that if Cynthia continued to antagonize so many people his chances of higher promotion must suffer.

He had tried to speak to Cynthia to explain the need to be tactful but this had proved to be impossible. She had demanded to know if he really were asking her to gain his promotion by crawling to a lot of women who, by their every action, showed the lack of any background. If he had no pride, she had. If he thought she was going to . . .

On the cornerstone of his life there was written in large letters, DUTY. No man could do more than his duty, no man should do less. So it never occurred to him that he had any choice in the matter: if either his marriage or his chances of promotion had to suffer, then it had to be the latter.

He had retired a captain. He had been sad that he had failed to attain flag rank, Cynthia had been bitter. They had found it difficult to settle down in retirement in England. The weather was bad, the permissive society upset them for very different reasons (a man could not learn to do his duty when all was permitted: sex was a dirty subject), and they made few friends because each of them, again for different reasons, found it difficult to be in sympathy with people whose standards were becoming more and more materialistic. She had decided that the only thing to do was to live abroad. After reading a book, which painted the island in words of gold, she had decided that they would live in Mallorca.

Before the final decision had been implemented he had pointed out certain facts. They were living in rented property and had no house to sell to raise the capital to buy one in Mallorca. During his career he'd managed to save only a little capital and he would, therefore, have to commute part of his pension and that might prove tricky. She had merely remarked, acidly, that since Spain was so much cheaper than England they would at least be able to enjoy the illusion of the kind of graceful living to which she had been accustomed before her marriage.

Prices of houses in Mallorca had proved to be higher than he had expected from reading advertisements in the Sunday papers—largely because she had insisted that they live in the most expensive part of Llueso, itself the most expensive area on the island, and had refused to be in any of the urbanizacions ('I have never lived in a housing estate before and am not going to start doing so now.'). They found a small bungalow in the Huerta of Llueso which was only just outside their price range. In the summer, when they bought it, it looked reasonably attractive: or at least as reasonably attractive as any other locally designed bungalow. But in the first winter they discovered that the flat roofs leaked, rising damp galloped up the walls, the electrical wiring was a cat's-cradle of dangerous improvisation, and the plumbing was a bad, i.e. smelly, joke. What they had not been told was that the bungalow had been built by a waiter in his spare time. Rockford accepted all the problems with wry amusement: Cynthia met them with shrill complaint and rapidly came to hate the island, the islanders, and most of their fellow expatriates.

Inflation reached the island. A bottle of brandy—the index by which the British measured the degree of inflation—rose nearly fourfold in price. Maids asked six times as much per hour. All but the cheapest cuts of meat became a luxury . . . Because he had commuted part of his pension, the remaining part increased proportionally and not by the total amount by which pensions were raised. Their standard of living dropped, at first slowly, then more rapidly. He dutifully accepted what the fates had ordained: she railed against the fates and against

him, castigating him for having dragged her out to the
Godforsaken island when it had been obvious to anyone
with an ounce of common sense that inflation was going
to make life impossible . . .

People who knew them were astonished that he invariably treated her with good humour, kindness, and
respect, no matter how bitchy she was to him or how
embarrassed he became by her behaviour towards others.
What they failed to realize was that as her husband it was
his duty to treat her with good humour, kindness, and
respect.

He went into the post office in Llueso and joined the
queue who patiently waited — it was no good being impatient — to collect their letters. He was wearing a casual
cotton shirt outside linen trousers, yet despite such
anonymous informality he was unmistakably a man of the
sea. Perhaps it was the way his light blue eyes would suddenly focus on distant horizons, or because the skin about
them was so wrinkled from squinting against the glare
of the sun on the sea, or maybe it was merely his bluff,
hearty, friendly appearance.

Eventually, he reached the single counter. 'Morning,'
he said in Spanish. 'Any mail for me?' Spaniards often
thought he was speaking Portuguese, but at the post
office they had learned to understand him.

The letters were stored in racks of pigeonholes. All
those in 'R' were taken out and carefully sorted through:
a couple were extracted and handed to him. A quick
check showed that one of these was for a man called
Thompson. He handed it back. The postal clerk was
totally unsurprised by his own error.

Rockford went out into the street and stood in the
shade. The letter was from his brother and he'd been expecting it for almost a month now. He used his forefinger
to rip open the envelope, brought out the letter, and read
it. 'Bugger!' he said. He put the letter back in the

envelope and the envelope in his trouser pocket. Then he walked along the road and into the square.

The land on which the square stood sloped to the south, but part of it had been raised to provide a level surface and on this a number of tables and chairs were set out in front of a bar. He walked towards one of the unoccupied tables. A couple nearby called to him to join them, but he shook his head and sat. He wanted to think.

After a while, a waiter came to the table and in his execrable Spanish he asked for a brandy and soda. It cost him less than it would a tourist, but slightly more than if he had been a Mallorquin. He drank slowly, immersed in his thoughts, and remained at the table for some time after he'd finished. Then he stood and left, striding off at a rate which made little concession to the heat, past shuttered windows and bead-curtained doors.

Nearing the end of the two kilometre walk, he passed the gateway of Ca Na Nadana. The diving-board of the kidney-shaped pool was just visible. He felt the sweat roll down his back and his chest. If envy were one of the seven deadly sins, then he was sinning heavily right then . . .

When he stepped into the sitting-room of his own bungalow, Cynthia said: 'The oven won't heat up properly.'

'I'd better see if a clean-up of the burners will do any good, then.'

'And the water pump's sounding funny.'

'It's probably only vibration, but I'll check it.'

'Did you get the beans?'

'Er . . . no. Afraid I forgot. I'll go back and get some.'

'It's too late.' She had been standing by the French windows which looked out on to the tiny back garden, as dusty and as tired-looking as the front one. She turned. 'You'll have to go without.'

'No bean feast today, eh?'

She said coldly: 'I've had a very trying morning,

Phillip. Would it be too much to ask you not to be stupid just for a little?'

'Sorry, old thing . . . Have a drink to cheer yourself up?'

'I don't want a drink.'

'Well, I do: that walk's dried me right out. Are you sure you won't change your mind?'

'I am not in the habit of changing my mind.'

True enough, he thought. He opened the lid of the chest and brought out the brandy bottle. He went through to the kitchen.

The hatch was up. 'I saw Dolly this morning, leaving her place,' she said, her voice sharper than ever.

As he took a tray of ice from the refrigerator, he wondered how many times a week she stared enviously at Ca Na Nadana, clearly visible from the bungalow.

'She's bought another new car.'

He realized that the malfunctioning oven and water pump were symptoms of her discontent.

'She only had the last one for a year. It's ridiculous getting another new one already.'

He poured himself out a very generous brandy, added soda and three cubes of ice, raised his glass, and drank.

'She does it to show off. Flaunting her money.'

'I don't suppose she's really doing that, old girl.'

'What would you know about women like her?'

He jiggled the glass, to send the ice cubes swirling round it.

'This car's so big it won't be able to get round some of the corners in the village.'

He sighed, left the kitchen, returned to the sitting-room.

'Her husband probably was a scrap metal merchant, but at least he left her enough money to be able to live decently.'

He sat on the settee and stretched out his legs. 'I'm sorry I'm not rich and dead,' he said cheerfully.

'That is a ridiculous thing to say . . . Since you forgot the beans, you're going to have to put up with a scrap lunch.'

'That's fine by me.'

'In other words, you don't appreciate what I do for you enough to care?' She walked the length of the sitting-room to the very short passage and turned off that into the kitchen. She spoke to him through the opened hatch-way. 'I suppose you did manage to remember to go to the post?'

'Yes.'

'Was there any mail?'

It would have been easy to say there had been none. But a man did not lie to his wife. 'Just one letter, for me.'

'Who was it from?' She often treated her own mail as secret: she always demanded to know everything about his.

'Garry.'

'How is he?' Her tone became slightly less scratchy. Garry Rockford lived in a large house, had a smart with-it wife, and drove a Jaguar.

'He says they're all very fit.'

Something about the way he spoke made her look through the hatchway and she noticed his expression. 'Has something happened?'

He finished his drink. 'Look, old girl, there's something I've got to tell you.'

She walked out of the kitchen and into the sitting-room, where she stood in the centre, directly facing him. 'Well?'

'Some time ago, he wrote to tell me his business wasn't doing so well. The recession and inflation have knocked an awful lot of businesses . . .'

'You never told me this.'

She had been in England when he'd received the letter: he hadn't mentioned it when she'd returned. There was a

vital difference between telling a lie and merely keeping
silent. He fiddled with the glass which he still held. 'He
was certain the trouble was only temporary and that a
spot of cash would tide him over. Wanted to know if I
could possibly help him.'

'Naturally you said you couldn't?'

He looked up at her, hoping she'd understand. 'He
promised to pay it back within six months.'

'Pay what back?'

'The money I lent him.'

'You . . . you lent him money?'

He nodded.

'How could you?'

'I sold some of the government stock.' By the time he'd
retired, he'd managed to save some money, despite all her
extravagances. When she had decided they would move
to Mallorca he had spoken to a friend who was an account-
ant and had explained that he needed to buy a house
and yet have sufficient income to live reasonably comfort-
ably, how was he to do this? His friend had suggested that
he commute part of his pension, buy the house, and then
invest all remaining capital in high yielding tax free
(when living abroad) government stock. He had done this
and after buying Ca'n Bispo his investments had, when
added to his reduced pension, happily come to slightly
more than the full pension. What no one had then foreseen had been that inflation would come roaring in on the
backs of the oil sheikhs and that it would need very few
years to prove how wrong in the long term his friend's
advice had been.

'How much did you lend him?' Her lips formed a
straight line: a small pulse in her neck had become visible.

'What he asked for — five thousand pounds.'

'When are the six months up?'

'They were up a month ago.'

'Then he's paid you back?'

'No.'

'Why not?'

'Things at home are still terribly difficult. He's sorry, but it's going to take a little longer.'

'He's got to repay you now. D'you hear—now!'

'Look, old girl, he just can't.'

'I don't care what ridiculous excuses he's made.'

He sighed.

'If he won't, you must sue him.'

He was startled. 'I couldn't do that.'

'Why not?'

'He's my brother.'

She looked at him with scorn.

CHAPTER 4

Matas was sixty and at times looked well over seventy: a lifetime of working on the land, often bent double and in a heat which sucked the last drop of moisture out of a man even before he had stopped work for his merienda, had left his once stocky frame bowed and his skin tanned to the texture and appearance of old, cracked leather.

'I asked you to put those chrysanthemums there,' said Dolly, keeping her voice low and sweet as she pointed.

He shook his head. They had, over the past years of a tumultuous relationship, evolved a method of communication which was a miracle of tongues. She spoke almost no Spanish and he spoke no English whatsoever, yet they managed to understand each other sufficiently well to be infuriated frequently and irritated always.

'I told you very clearly last Friday to plant the chrysanthemums in that bed so there'd be some colour in the early autumn.'

He chewed at something as he leaned against the heavily corrugated trunk of an almond tree.

'I want them dug up from here and put there.'

'That's impossible.'

Her voice became a shade less sweet. 'It is perfectly possible and you're to do it.'

He hawked and spat, knowing how much she loathed his doing that. 'It's impossible,' he repeated, with growing satisfaction.

'If you can't do what I tell you, there's little point in your continuing to work here.'

He stared up at the mountains.

'Either you move them now or you finish working for me.'

'Impossible,' he said for the third time.

'Very well.' There were now two spots of red (not artificial) on her cheeks. She hated the Mallorquins for their independence and could never understand why, since they loved money to the exclusion of most other things, they could not understand that to earn it they must be ready to lose their independence. 'I'll pay you to the end of the week.'

He shrugged his shoulders. 'It's all the same to me what you do.'

She left and crossed the lawn to the covered patio.

He had collected up a number of stones from the flower-bed and put these in a rubber trug—one of the two-handled carrying containers which were used for a hundred and one jobs, from building houses to collecting seaweed. He tipped the trug on to its side and spilled out the stones, then kicked them about the flower-bed with his shoe. That done, he went round the house to the garage and put the trug with the rest of the gardening tools, kept beyond the second car and up against the wall. He picked up a plastic carrier bag, in which he had earlier packed a couple of kilos of tomatoes picked off the plants when certain no one was watching him, put the bag in the wooden box fixed on the back of his Mobylette and carefully arranged a piece of sacking to cover the bag. He wheeled the Mobylette out into the drive and started it.

He rode the kilometre to the eastern side of Llueso, crossed the first bridge over the torrente which was dust dry, and took the third turning on the left.

His wife was sitting on a chair in the road immediately outside the front door of their house, crocheting a bed-spread which would form part of their daughter's dowry. With her sat the woman who lived next door. Neither said anything to him as he wheeled the Mobylette into what had been the stable and left it propped against a wall. He picked up the bag of tomatoes and took it through to the kitchen. Then he sat in the sitting-room, dim because it was without windows, and thought about nothing very much.

After a while—he'd no idea how long a time had elapsed—his wife came through.

'She fired me,' he said.

She nodded, continued on through to the kitchen.

He shouted: 'I fixed things so the señora fired me.'

'So now you've no work to do?' she shouted back. 'Then you can mend the chest-of-drawers.'

Since when had he been a carpenter? . . . What fools the rich foreigners were! Had he gone to the señora and said, 'Señora, the price of everything has gone up yet again. Because of this, the builders have been given more money, the electricians have been given more money, and surely it is only right that you should give me more for the very great work I do?' she would have refused to increase his wages. She'd have said she couldn't afford to pay him any more money. Couldn't afford to, when she lived in a palace, wasted a fortune on watering grass which wasn't even fed to animals, and bought new cars so often he'd lost count of their numbers! . . . So he had decided what would annoy her the most and then had done that thing. As planned, she had lost her temper and had fired him. In a few days' time, but certainly not more than four in such heat, the grass would begin to look tired and the plants would droop because no one would be able to make the automatic sprinklers work (they'd never find that piece of wood in the back of the control panel) and the señora would panic because if she truly loved anything other than herself it was her garden . . . And either Victoriana or Ana would come along to this house and say, 'You old bastard, come and make the sprinklers work. The señora says to tell you it was all a misunderstanding and she'll up your money to five hundred pesetas an hour . . .'

He knew a slow, warm pleasure. Life had become good in the last few years. Those days of poverty, when a man could not feed his own family since there was no work, and those days of terror when a man was forced to take up arms and then might be shot because he was fighting for the wrong side, although he had had neither choice nor the knowledge on which to make a choice, had become a distant, confused memory. Now, there was plenty of money to buy food. His wife did not have to spend all her days in the fields, breaking her body to earn a few pesetas. Their daughter, Rosa, could both read and write, which was a miracle because neither he nor his wife could do either . . . Rosa was grown tall and very beautiful and the young men were like bees around the honey pot. (Let one of them take a step too far and his cojones would be forfeit.) One day she would have a novio who would marry her and the wedding feast would be at a restaurant: mountains of food and barrels of liquor. She would take to her marriage bed her virginity, two crocheted counterpanes, sheets, blankets, and presents galore. As much as any princess could have taken to her marriage bed when he was young . . .

Perhaps he would demand from the señora five hundred and twenty-five pesetas an hour before he agreed to return to Ca Na Nadana. The future was going to require much money.

Steven Kenley turned into the drive of Ca Na Nadana and thought, once again, that it must have been quite difficult to design a house in such ostentatiously bad taste. He parked near the double garage, crossed the drive to the front door, and rang the bell. Ana opened the door. He liked her. She had the kind of face in which ugliness became almost a virtue, perhaps because she was always happy.

She showed him into the sitting-room, then left to call the señora. He remained standing and stared through one of the side windows at the pool. Mark Erington was swimming with a stylish, powerful crawl. He could be an amusing man: but it was impossible to forget the position he occupied in this house.

Dolly, wearing a trouser suit and managing not to look ridiculous in it, a diamond horse brooch on her bosom, a double rope of pearls about her neck, diamond and ruby rings on her fingers, entered the room, followed by a panting Lulu. 'Good morning, Steven, how nice to see you.'

He murmured the usual pleasantries and told her how his wife was as they both sat. An honest man, he would never have said that he liked her. But she had helped him when he'd been in trouble and for that he was most grateful and, old-fashioned in outlook, for him gratitude became a fair substitute for friendship.

'I hope you don't mind my calling in like this?' he asked.

'Of course I don't,' she answered. 'You know this is open house to my friends.'

'I came because it's the twenty-third.'

'The twenty-third—is that in some way significant?'

Kenley naively accepted that she had forgotten. 'It's six months ago today you lent me the money and I promised to start repaying you now.'

'Oh, that!' she said, with indifference.

'I always stick to my word.' Lettie often teased him about his righteousness, but he was proud to know that in a world of rapidly declining values, his remained fixed.

'I know you do, which is why I didn't have the slightest hesitation in helping.' She looked at her watch. 'I think we might have a drink, don't you?'

He was the kind of man who would never drink before midday, come hell or high water. 'Not for me, thanks all the same.' He was not looking at her and so he missed her brief expression of annoyance. He coughed. 'I want to thank you again for your wonderful kindness.' He knew he sounded stiff, but discussing money always embarrassed him.

'It was absolutely nothing.'

At the time it had been a miracle. Lettie had tripped over a step in their house—traversed hundreds of times before without trouble—and had fallen on to a wooden box. Her thigh-bone had been badly fractured. Rushed into one of the Palma clinics, she had undergone a long and complicated operation immediately, and a second one a fortnight later. Even before the second operation, he had received the bill for the previous one and for the first week's stay in the clinic. The total had appalled him. Of course, Lettie and he had held medical insurance, but they'd never been very well off, they'd always been healthy, and somehow he had failed to appreciate how far behind the potential costs the cover of the insurance had fallen. (There was, it was true, a so-called reciprocal agreement between the Spanish and British authorities concerning national health, but to the British expatriates it was difficult to identify even a hint of reciprocity about it.) He had gone to his bank to borrow money and they had been very pleasant as they had pointed out that since he didn't own any property in Spain—he and Lettie had only a life lease on their house—he could offer them no security and therefore they could not help him. After the second operation, the clinic had, with florid Spanish politeness, pointed out that by now a great deal of money was owed to them and if he wished his wife to continue to receive the very necessary treatment he must surely understand that they must be paid. He had gone to the British Consulate to see how they could help him: they told him, in that official manner which is not to be confused with rudeness, that they could not help him in any way because he was not presently destitute. Desperate, he had swallowed a lifetime's principle and approached one of two of their wealthier friends to ask them to lend him the money. He discovered the worth of some friendships and failed to borrow a peseta. Then, so frantic nothing was too ridiculous to try, he had come to Dolly: she had lent him what he asked.

'I've brought you a cheque,' he said.

'How very kind of you, Steven.'

He stood and took from the inside pocket of his light-weight jacket—he never dressed casually when visiting—his wallet from which he brought out a cheque. 'I'm afraid it's not for quite as much as I had hoped, but I've had to have a physiotherapist along three times a week to treat Lettie and he does charge such a lot of money.'

'They're all robbers. My hairdresser in Palma is now charging me four thousand pesetas.'

He crossed the carpet and handed her the cheque.

She read the figure. 'And this is the interest, isn't it? I'm afraid I haven't worked out the figure, but I'm sure you're right.'

He stared at her. 'Interest?'

She might not have heard him. 'Although to be truthful, you know it does seem just a little bit less than I'd expected.'

'But . . . but that's repaying you a proportion of what you lent me. We never talked about interest.'

'But Steven, dear, we did agree, didn't we, that the only way of managing this between friends was to make it a business agreement?'

'Yes, but . . .' He had signed a statement to say that she had lent him 310,000 pesetas. Until now, he had presumed that that alone had been what she had meant by a 'business agreement'.

'When one borrows money under a business agreement one always has to pay a little bit of interest.'

He stared at her bejewelled fingers as she stroked the snuffling Lulu. His mind was threatening to panic. Suppose she asked for five per cent? On 310,000 pesetas that would come to 15,500 pesetas a year. Not very much, perhaps — except that their budget was now stretched to their last peseta . . .

She said sweetly: 'I think twenty per cent would be very fair, don't you?'

'Twenty?' he said hoarsely.

'I know you'll appreciate that as this is a business agreement I have to be partially recompensed for the loss I've suffered in not having the money working.'

'But I thought . . .' He'd thought she'd been wanting to help him in his desperate need. Twenty per cent. 62,000 pesetas a year. 31,000 already owed for the past six months. More than the cheque he had just handed to her . . .

She said: 'I really am sorry that it's so high, but it's all the fault of those beastly socialists.'

'But . . . but the banks here aren't charging that much.'

'Didn't you tell me, though, that the banks wouldn't

lend you any money?'

'It's money I had to have for Lettie. She was in hospital . . .'

'D'you remember, Steven, you did tell me all about that? As I've always said, you can't spend too much on health. After all, once you've lost it, it's gone for ever.'

'I . . . I don't think I can afford twenty per cent.'

'Oh dear, that is difficult, isn't it? After all, you did agree to make it a business agreement and we typed out that little note to make certain. And I know that if you'd borrowed the money in London you'd have had to pay more than twenty per cent . . .'

CHAPTER 5

Erington heard a car door slam and then the car drive off. What a soft fool Kenley was, he thought. Letting her browbeat him into paying twenty per cent on the grounds that he'd given his word. Didn't he know that the Victorian age was over and that the only thing to do now was to worry about number one? Erington stood — he'd moved on to the patio to hear what was said — and looked through the nearest window. Dolly was still on the settee. Call her what you would, you had to hand it to her! Put her to work in the City and watch the sharks swim to cover.

He went inside. 'Who was that who's just gone?'

'Steven. He called in to say hullo.'

'And when you offered him a drink I bet he refused it.' He mimicked Kenley's earnest, pedantic voice. 'I never drink before midday. My dear father told me that only alcoholics and loose women did that . . . D'you know, I've never understood what Pater meant by loose women.' He leaned over and kissed her neck. 'You're looking a million dollars.'

'Flatterer,' she said archly.

'But not flattering to deceive.'

'No?'

'Darling, do you think I would ever try to deceive you?'

'I hope not,' she answered. Her tone was not as light as it had been.

'I may not be bright, but I know my limitations.' He nuzzled her neck for a little, then stood up. 'I thought I'd just nip out to the post. Is there anything you want?'

'Tell Ana to go to the post office. You stay here and have a little drinkie with Dolly.'

'I'd really love to, but I also want to buy a lottery ticket.'

'She can get that as well.'

'But it's bad luck to get someone else to buy it for me.'

'I've never heard that before.'

'Which is why you've never won a prize worth much.'

He smiled, said he wouldn't be a second longer than necessary, and left before she could object any further. He went through the kitchen, winking at Victoriana on the way, and out into the garage. He settled in the driving seat of the blood red open Seat 124 Sport, whose hood was folded back, started the engine, blipped it a couple of times, and then backed out at speed: he was a skilled driver, though not as skilled as he believed.

As he drove past fields in which crops were being intensively grown, thanks to the plentiful supply of water which came down in stone channels from a spring up in the foothills of the mountains, the wind curled round the sides of the raked windscreen to flick at his hair and ease away a little of the heat of the burning sun. His thoughts were confused. Ever since he'd been old enough to judge what kind of a place the world was, he'd rightly prided himself on being smart. Yet now, when he'd everything to lose, he was in danger of acting so stupidly . . .

He crossed the Laraix road and entered the village—so

called, despite its 10,000 inhabitants—and drove through
the maze of narrow streets to the public call-box on the
west side. He parked in front of a carpenter's workshop
and as he tried to make sense of his thoughts there came
from inside the workshop brief bursts of tooth-tingling
noise as a band saw bit into wood.

One thing was for certain. However much Dolly was
enamoured of him, if ever she became convinced that he
was betraying her she'd throw him out of the house so
quickly he wouldn't even have time to think up an excuse.
So why risk such a catastrophe? Why put in jeopardy all
that he had so carefully earned for himself . . . ?

All cats were the same under the skin. And he'd known
women more beautiful, much more sensual, than Carol.
Yet here he was, parked outside a telephone kiosk,
hesitating about phoning her to ask if she'd have a meal
with him—knowing this would be to risk everything.
In God's name, why? Mockingly, contemptuously, he
answered his own question. He, who had taught himself
that good and evil were the same thing, only seen from
different financial viewpoints, was so strongly attracted to
her because it was impossible not to realize that she would
always recognize and differentiate between the two and
unhesitatingly choose good. It was this quality of judgement which so attracted him, as the negative of one
magnet was attracted by the positive of another . . . Far
from being emotionally self-sufficient, as he had so
prided himself, he was like a little boy on his first day at
school, desperately longing to be noticed by the teacher so
that he might gain her approval. A bloody fool.

He left the car and crossed the pavement to the kiosk.

CHAPTER 5

Rockford, telephone receiver to his ear, roared with laughter. 'I've got to remember that one. Did I tell you about the man with a lisp trying to offer a box of matches to a beautiful young lady . . . Oh, I did . . . See you both on Sunday evening for the yardarm sherrymony, then. Thanks for ringing.' He replaced the receiver. 'That was Basil.'

Cynthia did not look up from the copy of *Country Life* she was reading.

'How about this? Why did the pheasant cross the road?'

Her lips tightened.

'Because it wanted to get to the other ride.'

'I really don't know how you can be quite so infantile.'

'Retarded development,' he admitted cheerfully. 'By the way, Basil's asked us to drinks on Sunday evening.'

She clipped her words, as she did when she was annoyed. 'I am not going there next Sunday, or any other Sunday, to suffer that ghastly wife of his.'

'I suppose she is a bit loud.'

'The correct word is common.'

'But she can be amusing fun.'

'Certainly, if your conception of fun is a barmaid's crudity.'

He ran his fingers through his hair. 'Bit of a problem. Thing is, I've just told Basil we will go.'

'Then you'll have to ring back and tell him that irrespective of what you do, I certainly have no intention of going.'

He hesitated, then said: 'Couldn't you turn a blind eye to some of the things she says? She's not really a bad sort, you know: quite the opposite, in fact. Done a lot for some

people and hasn't gone round the place shouting about it.
There was that elderly English widow who fell off her bike
and broke her leg and couldn't afford any help in the
house. Mabel went to her flat every day and cooked a
midday meal for her . . .'

'I have been told that people of Mabel's background
are very attached to a communal life . . . Next time you
receive an invitation, perhaps you could take the trouble
to consult me first before you accept?'

He crossed to the bookcase and picked up his pipe.

'If you must smoke, Phillip, could you please not leave
your things around to make a mess. There will be ash
everywhere.'

He tamped down the half-burned tobacco with his
forefinger, put the pipe in his mouth, struck a match,
and lit the tobacco. He looked around for an ashtray and
saw a brass one on an occasional table.

She said, as he walked to the table: 'I polished that
ashtray this morning, but I suppose you'd better use it if
you must.'

He put the used match back in the box of matches.

'Phillip, have you received a letter from your brother in
the past couple of days?'

'You know I haven't.'

'All I know is that you haven't mentioned one.'

She was never going to forget that episode, he thought.

'You ought to have heard from him by now.'

'It's still early days with the post between here and
home taking even longer than usual. I reckon the mail's
being sent by no boat to China.'

'Phillip! Will you please stop that.'

'Sorry.'

'You told him you must have the money back?'

'Yes.'

'Immediately?'

'Yes.'

'I still can't begin to understand what possessed you to lend it to him.'

He drew on the pipe, to find it had gone out. He took the box of matches from his pocket, hesitated, then said: 'I think I'll go for a walk.'

'In this heat?'

'It's not too bad, really. Not like Singapore that year . . .'

'Must you go on and on, repeating the same stories?'

'It's old age.'

'It's thoughtlessness.'

He walked across to the very short passage to the front door.

'Phillip, I've been going through the invitation list for our party. I've decided not to ask the Moores. His behaviour last year was quite disgraceful.'

'As a matter of fact, old girl . . .' He turned, filling the passage with his comfortable bulk.

'There's no point in trying to find excuses for him. A gentleman holds his liquor: if he doesn't, he's not a gentleman.'

'What I was going to say was, I don't think we ought to have a party.'

'Not have our annual cocktail-party?'

'It always comes to quite a bit, doesn't it?'

'Quite a bit of what?'

'Money. I mean, we never buy any of the booze out of the barrel as lots of people do to cut the costs . . .'

'I am not going to start treating my guests like a lot of peasants.'

'The better stuff from the barrel is exactly the same as the bottled . . .'

'I really am not interested, Phillip.'

He sighed, turned, and left the house to go for a walk along the meandering dirt tracks, to greet any Mallorquin he met in his execrable Spanish, to appreciate the beauty

of the countryside which was both barren and lush, and
to enjoy the satisfaction of knocking out his pipe against
the heel of his shoe and not giving a damn where the wind
scattered the ash.

CHAPTER 6

The days became hotter, the landscape, where there was
no irrigation, more burned up. At dusk, the mountains
would appear to shimmer as they began to release some of
the heat which they had soaked up during the day and
immediately above them the sky would purple before all
colour disappeared.

'It's too hot,' complained Dolly. 'Turn up the air-
conditioning. And do switch off the programme. I can't
stand it.'

Erington switched off the television which had been
showing a video tape recording of the Edinburgh Tattoo.
He then went over to the air-conditioning unit, set low on
the wall, and moved the control dial to its maximum set-
ting.

'It sounds terribly noisy tonight. Did you remember to
tell the service man it was noisy?'

'I did. He checked it over and said nothing was wrong.'

'He obviously didn't know anything about it,' she said
fretfully.

'Don't you know the definition of a modern service
engineer? He's the man who says your machine's in
wonderful nick the day before it blows up.' He noted that
she didn't smile. Softly, softly, he told himself. Something
had got her into one of her bitchy moods . . .

There was a silence which she broke abruptly. 'You
were out in my car the other evening.' It was 'his' car
when things were sweet: 'her' car when they were sour.

Obviously, she had learned about his evening with Carol. Goddamn it, on this island you couldn't blow your nose without half a dozen people 'knowing' you'd got a cold. Yet he'd chosen a restaurant deep in the mountains behind Palma where few foreigners ate . . .

'Did you go to the casino?'

'You know I did, Dolly.'

'Who did you take?'

'No one, of course.'

'You took that woman you met in the square.'

'What woman? . . . Oh, I suppose you mean Carol? As a matter of fact, I haven't seen her from that day to this.'

'Liar.'

'Dolly, my love, would Markie ever lie to you?'

'If you thought you'd get away with it.'

'Knowing how smart you are, d'you think I'd even try?'

'I know you took her. You were seen with her.'

'At the casino? No way.'

'In my car, driving back.'

He laughed. 'The mystery's suddenly resolved!'

'Then you admit you were with her?'

'I admit I drove back from Palma with a blonde.'

'It was Carol,' she said thickly.

'I suppose that could have been her name.' Expertly, he judged just how far he dare try her temper.

'What d'you mean, might have been?'

He didn't answer, but said: 'I don't know about you, but I could really attack another drink.'

'Answer me.'

He crossed to her side. 'You do leap to the most terrible conclusions.' He sat and reached for her left hand. She moved it. Smiling, he leaned over until he could imprison it. 'I promise you there's absolutely no need to get so upset. I went to the casino on my own, concentrated on my system for winning a fortune at roulette and ignored whatever feminine pulchritude there was around—easy enough, when I'm coming back to you, darling—and succeeded in losing all my money in just under two hours. So then I started back for here and was just leaving the outskirts of Palma when a blonde thumbed a lift. It was pretty late and I reckoned it was a bit dangerous for her to do that sort of thing because there's no knowing who'd pick her up, so I stopped and asked her where she wanted to go.'

'I'm not a fool. You picked her up because she was pretty.'

He chuckled. 'If that was my real reason, I was well punished for my sins! She might have looked all right at a distance, but seen close to . . .'

'Where did you take her?'

Dolly hadn't said where Carol and he had been seen together. 'Down to the Port.'

'Why d'you go there?'

'Because that was where she was staying. Surely you wouldn't have wanted me to leave her at the side of the main road, having to thumb a lift down to the Port in the middle of the night?'

'She wasn't bothered earlier on.'

'Now, now, sweetie, show a little charity. It was just that having once picked her up, stupidly I felt responsible for seeing she arrived back safely.' He watched her face closely and finally became satisfied that he'd been believed. Bloody close, he thought. But there wasn't a situation that a quick mind and a ready tongue couldn't talk its way out of. 'Now, how about that little drinkie?' Fill her up with cognac and she'd forget the whole affair.

They slept in separate bedrooms. 'I don't want the staff to get the wrong idea.' As a connoisseur of hypocrisy, he rated that very highly. But it was an arrangement which suited him because it meant that he had a room in which he could be on his own.

He switched off the air-conditioning: the room was quite cool enough and if the machine ran through the night he'd wake up with a sore throat and a painfully dry nose. He went through to the en suite bathroom: maroon-coloured tiles from floor to ceiling, rich gold-coloured tiles on the floor, egg-shaped, deep blue bath seven feet along its greater axis, gold-plated taps, marble sur-rounds, matching bidet, WC, and twin handbasins, recessed cabinets with interior strip lighting . . . A sharp contrast to the only bathroom in the house which he'd lived in until he left home.

He returned to the bedroom. It was twenty feet long and fifteen wide—who the hell could work out anything in metres?—and it could have slept a whole family in comfort. Built-in cupboards lined one wall. On the tiled floor were two matching Ladik prayer carpets with their stylized design of tulips. On the wall facing the bed, hanging between the two windows, was a painting of two horses, one a dark bay and the other a grey, by Stubbs. The bed was king size. The cover had been removed, carefully folded, and placed on one of the three needle-worked chairs. The lilac-coloured, hand-embroidered, Irish linen sheet—no blankets—had been turned down at one corner and his silk sulu—about which Victoriana had made more than one ribald comment—was on the top pillow. On one of the matching bedside tables there was a glass and an insulated flask containing iced water. Set in the wall was a bell-push. Summon the maid for whatever you wanted—within reason.

He undressed, wrapped the colourful sulu about his waist, pulled back the top sheet, lay down, and looked at his watch—a gold Piaget. It was nearly midnight.

He thought about Carol and how she'd unwittingly forced him to listen to his yearnings instead of his com-mon sense. Who'd seen him with her and rushed to pass the news on to Dolly? Someone who felt personally aggrieved because the rewards for virtue were obviously so much less than those for vice? What if that someone had been able to make a definite identification so that Dolly would have known for certain his passenger had been Carol . . . ?

He was smart, so he'd never risk taking Carol out again. Yet even as he reached this decision, he remembered the strange, dream-drifting pleasure it had been to be with her, to listen to her laughter, to share in her warm acceptance of the world exactly as it was . . . Could he really forgo such pleasure? Was his decision really final? He swore. Surely there had to be some way of reconciling the irreconcilable? Couldn't he continue to enjoy the life of luxury which Dolly provided, yet at the same time see Carol again because she offered him something else, something which until now he had not recognized how badly he wanted?

CHAPTER 7

They swam around an anchored schooner, with brilliant blue hull and a carved figurehead. Between them and the shore a ski-boat crossed, towing an expert skier: a windsurfer, ill at ease even though the wind was so light, failed to keep his balance and fell back into the sea: a small catamaran, her sail as many coloured as Joseph's coat, ghosted along with a man at the helm and a woman, proudly topless, sitting against the mast.

'Race you to the shore,' said Carol.

'What d'you want: twenty yards' start?' asked Trent.

'Big head.'

'OK. Scratch for both and loser buys ices.'

Her crawl was stylish, his was not, but the powerful strokes of his arms pulled him through the water at speed.

When within fifty yards of the beach he slowed down, only to discover that she had done the same.

She laughed. 'I read your thoughts. Can't have her buying me an ice-cream so I'll pretend to lose . . . We'll have to declare the race a dead heat or we'll spend the rest of the afternoon trying to be last home.'

'Very sensible. More especially as the ice-cream man's moved too far away.'

They swam lazily to the shore and crossed the sand to their towels, on which they lay down. The heat of the sun induced a drifting weightlessness and she was half asleep when he said: 'Did you have a meal with him?'

'Who's him?'

'Who d'you think? Lover boy.'

'Mark? We had dinner together, yes.'

'At some five-star hotel?'

'At a little restaurant up in the mountains near Gallilea. There was a balcony where after the meal one could sit out and have coffee and just see part of Palma bay. The moon was out and the sea was all speckled silver . . . It was so beautiful.'

'He didn't choose it because it was beautiful, but because he reckoned there wasn't any chance of meeting the old bitch there.'

'You could be so wrong.'

'That's possible, but I'd never bet on it.'

She moved and sat with her knees drawn up, her chin on her knees, and her arms about her legs. 'He's really a different person from what you seem to think he is.'

'I've been too generous?'

'Come on, relax. It's your day off, there isn't a cloud in the sky, and we've had a wonderful swim. Stop imitating a bear with a sore head.'

'I can't stand the man.'

'I'd never have guessed that.'

'How in the hell can you bear to have anything to do

with him? A gigolo.'

'Does it really matter what he is?'

'Of course it damn well does.'

'He makes Dolly happy. Surely that's all that's important?'

'It all depends on your standards.'

'What makes you so certain yours are the right ones?'

'I know one thing for sure. A man stops being a man when he starts living off a woman.'

'Suppose there are good reasons for what he's doing?'

'There couldn't be any.'

'George . . . Why do you always get so hot under the collar about him?'

'I don't like gigolos.'

'I can think of many far worse kinds of people.'

'All right. So I don't like them either.'

She laughed. 'Some American once wrote a book on how to make friends. Would you like me to try and find you a copy?'

'Steve,' said Lettie Kenley, 'you'll just have to go and talk to her again.' She was a small woman with an impish look to her face and when she smiled, which normally was often, there was a hint of ready mockery about her mouth.

Kenley muttered something, then he got up from the patio chair and crossed to the nearest flower-bed which was filled with gazanias.

'Come on back here,' she said, in the same tone in which she had admonished their son when he had been small.

'Lots of weeds . . .'

'Come and sit down so that we can talk things over.'

He straightened up and the harsh sunshine picked out the signs of strain in his face. He had suddenly begun to look old, she thought with a brief, sharp surge of panic.

He bent and pulled up a length of creeping grass, slowly returned to the shade and the chair with the grass still in his hand. He began to twist it round his thumb and forefinger. Tim had always done that when uneasy or embarrassed, she thought, this time with the sad regret of a mother whose son and family lived a thousand miles away.

From across the urbanizacion came the shouts of people in the communal swimming pool: pop music blared out from the next-door house which had been rented by a French family: just along the road a number of children were playing a game which seemed to consist of screaming as loudly and for as long as possible. 'Appy 'Ampstead, some of the British residents—who could afford to live in different surroundings—called it.

'Originally, you quite definitely did not agree to pay her twenty per cent,' she said.

He shook his head.

'All you agreed was that the loan should be treated as a business deal. By that, you meant you'd acknowledge the debt in writing?'

'The trouble is, she obviously thought . . .'

'She's a bitch.' Lettie did not normally swear, but when she did she chose her words carefully. 'You can't tell me she doesn't know we have to watch every peseta we spend. So for someone in her financial position to ask for twenty per cent interest on money borrowed in an emergency is completely immoral.'

'I know it is. But that doesn't change anything.'

'It does for me.'

'It doesn't for me,' he said miserably.

'You are not going to pay her.'

'I don't see how I can get out of it. I promised . . .'

'If she's so besotted with money that she has to have some interest, you'll pay her five per cent and not a fraction more.'

'But if she thought that originally I was agreeing . . .'

'Are you scared of her?'

'Of course not.'

'Because if you are, I don't in the least mind telling her.'

'It's not that at all.'

'I know,' she said, suddenly sounding weary. 'It's because you always keep your word and if she thought you meant one thing and you failed to make it clear you didn't, because you were so worried, you feel obliged to carry out your side of the bargain as she conceived it . . . I suppose I ought to be proud you can be so honourable: but all I can think is that it's people like you who make life too easy for people like her.'

He had been winding and unwinding the grass about his thumb and forefinger and now it broke in the middle. After a brief, sideways, look at her, he stood.

'If we gave her twenty per cent,' she said, 'we'd never, ever be able to pay off the capital.'

He nodded, then walked round the side of the house. She thought that she shouldn't have pressed the matter so firmly because she'd only managed to add to his worries. But if that bitch of a woman thought she was going to get twenty per cent . . .

The staff at Ca Na Nadana, by gracious permission of Dolly, were allowed to use the swimming pool at certain times of the day. Erington sat out on the pool patio and watched Victoriana as she dog-paddled in the water.

'Come on in,' she called out, with the familiarity with which she — but never Ana — spoke to him when Dolly was not within earshot.

He stood, crossed to the diving-board, and executed a perfect running dive. When he came to the surface, she said: 'When are you going to show me how to swim properly?'

'Any time.'

'Then now?'

'First I have to teach you the movements.'

'Where?'

'On a bed is best.' It was an old joke, not yet grown stale.

She laughed. Like most Mallorquins, she had an earthy sense of humour and it was some little while before the subject was exhausted.

'What's the time?' she asked as she stood waist deep in the shallow end, conscious that her scantily covered breasts were standing proud.

'Coming up to eleven.'

'Then I'd better get out and do some work. The señora said she'd be back by twelve and I must make the bed and tidy up the bedroom before she gets here. I can't think how her bed gets so disturbed.' She tried to suggest wide-eyed innocence, but had to laugh coarsely. He made several suggestive movements. She scooped her right hand across the surface of the water to splash him.

'I thought she was out for lunch?' he said casually.

'Is that what she told you?' She looked at him out of the corner of her eyes. 'Maybe she thought she'd come back and surprise you?'

'Surprise me doing what?'

'I wouldn't know, would I?' She waded to the steps and climbed out.

'I suppose she's having her hair done.'

'On a Wednesday: in the village?'

'I was forgetting she'd only gone into Llueso.'

'Ana said something about her making an appointment to see Old Foxy.' She picked up a towel and began to dry her face and hair.

'Who's Old Foxy?'

'You don't know? Vives, the solicitor.'

He'd thought that Victoriana would have a very good

idea of where Dolly had gone, but had had to be cir-
cumspect in finding out. Victoriana was an inveterate
gossip. She began to tell him about Vives — how he had
come to be the richest man in the village — but his mind
was not on what she said. Dolly had been very coy that
morning, refusing to explain where she was going or why
and merely insisting that she had to be on her own. So
why hadn't she wanted him to know she intended to speak
to one of the local solicitors and why a local man when
normally she dealt with one in Palma?

'I'm going inside to change,' she said.

'Need any help?'

She tossed her head with scorn and walked off. But her
rate of walking appeared to slow as she approached the
patio.

Many of the tiled floors in Ca Na Nadana were carpeted,
as were the stairs, and bare feet made only the faintest of
noises, nevertheless he waited until one o'clock the next
morning before he left his bedroom. Dolly's room was further away from the stairs so he did not have to pass her
doorway — not that that would have mattered very much
because she'd taken a sleeping pill. Victoriana and Ana
slept on the other side of the house.

With the aid of a small pocket torch, he went down the
main stairs to the hall and then into the study. He shut
and locked the door, reached through the opened window
and unlatched the closed shutters. In an emergency —
although it was difficult to conceive an emergency — he
could escape through the window. He used his skeleton
key to pick the lock of the top drawer of the kneehole
desk. On top of the untidy mass of papers was a large
brown envelope. He opened this and inside found two
documents, each of two pages, the first in Spanish and
the second a translation in English: Dolly's will. He read
the translation. George Trent was to receive a pewter

cigarette case, carefully identified. The whole of the rest of her estate, situated in Spain and elsewhere in the world, was to go to Mark Erington.

At three-ten that afternoon, Dolly burped with genteel decorum. 'I'm so hot—I'm sure the air-conditioning isn't working properly—that I think I'll go and have a little lie-down.'

'Very sensible,' said Erington.

'I'm almost certain to be down by five, but just in case I'm not, be a sweet boy and wake me up.' She got up from the settee and walked with care to the doorway: she always drank a lot of wine with her meals.

Give them ten minutes, he thought, and both she and Lulu would be stretched out, snoring. He picked up his glass and went out to sit under the covered patio. He stared out at the colour-filled garden with its dramatic backdrop of harsh mountains under full sun. What was Dolly worth if one added together all her possessions? A million pounds? Two million? And except for a pewter cigarette case—and he was prepared to be charitable about that!—everything was left to him.

He sipped the last of the cognac. Lord and master of Ca Na Nadana: rich beyond the dreams of Crœsus. He'd give parties and all those high-nosed women who now took such great pains to show their scorn for him would come and drink his drink and be as nice as their burned-out souls allowed because there was no denying money, not even if one had been the wife of a district commissioner . . .

He watched a hoopoe, a swirl of colour in undulating flight, cross the lawn and settle by the side of one of the rose-beds. It bobbed its head and raised its crest. Cocky little bastard: acting as proud as if it had just inherited a fortune . . .

He had to keep Dolly contented. No matter what she

wanted, he must smilingly provide it. There had not been much room for pride before: there was none now. He must become totally indispensable because then she would not consider changing her will . . .

Carol? He lit a cigarette. His desire to be with her, to renew his soul by reference to hers, had become a luxury he couldn't begin to afford . . . Yet even as he recognized that fact, he experienced a bitter, almost overwhelming longing to see her again and he sensed that it would be all too easy to formulate the ultimate blasphemy, to hell with money . . . If only Dolly were suddenly to die, how perfectly that would solve everything. But Dolly, despite her drinking habits, despite the fact that she would never have admitted this, was remarkably healthy and unlikely to die for years . . . Unless she were killed. Unless he murdered her . . . It was a wistful thought, admitting the impossibility even as the possibility was formulated. He knew himself too well: at heart, he was a coward.

CHAPTER 8

Matas, recalled to work as he'd known he must be, put the plastic bag filled with tomatoes in the basket of his Mobylette and carefully covered the bag with the piece of sacking. He wheeled the bike past the red Seat 124 Sport, which he admired so much, and into the harsh sunshine where he pulled it back up on to its stand. He didn't immediately start the engine, but looked up at the large and ancient almond tree immediately facing the garage and studied the fruit. It was going to be a good year for almonds. In late August or early September, the crop of the fourteen almond trees on the land would be ripe and the senora would tell him to knock it down and to sell it, but would insist that the buyer must pay her direct.

Suspicious old bag. He'd sell to Reinaldo. Reinaldo would give her a thousand pesetas less than the true price and later would hand him five hundred. The rich foreigners thought they were smart, but in truth they were all simple.

He looked away from the almond tree and put his foot on the pedal, his finger round the compression lever, to start the engine and at that moment Dolly came out of the front door. 'I want a word with you,' she called out.

He took his foot off the pedal and stolidly waited. She came to a stop immediately in front of the bike. 'Do you remember me telling you something when you first started working here?' she asked in a bullying tone.

He shrugged his shoulders. What she needed was a man man enough to belt her until she learned to shut up.

'I said that on no account whatsoever were you to take anything from here without my express consent.'

He hawked and spat.

'What is in that basket?' She pointed at the wire basket on the front of the Mobylette.

'An old sack,' he muttered.

'What have you got underneath that?'

Events were moving too quickly for him.

Events moved even more quickly. She reached forward and pulled off the sack. She picked up the plastic bag and looked inside. 'My tomatoes!'

'No,' he retorted angrily.

'My tomatoes, bought with my money, grown on my land, watered with my water.' She returned the bag to the carrier, dropping it as if it were suddenly contaminated.

'Mine,' he said hoarsely. It was he who each year insisted on growing vegetables in one half-hidden corner of the garden because it was a criminal waste to grow nothing but flowers and grass. It was he who had hoed and dunged the soil, planted the plants, irrigated them, harvested the crop . . .

'You've been stealing my tomatoes day after day after day. And before that it was my beans. And before that my lettuces.'

'My tomatoes, my beans, my lettuces.'

'Don't be ridiculous. I warned you and you've chosen to pay no heed to my warning. So when you leave here today, do not bother to come back again.'

'What's that?'

'You're fired.'

'No,' he cried, aghast.

She looked at him, then turned and went back into the house. The front door shut behind her. Mother of God! he thought, she had been smiling. Bemused, he stared at the front door.

'What's up with you, then?' asked Victoriana pertly, as she came round the corner of the garage, a bucket in her hand. When he made no answer, she became worried. 'Here, you're not ill, are you?'

He finally turned and looked at her. 'She . . . she's been and sacked me!'

She put the bucket down. Her brown eyes were alive with delighted curiosity.

'She can't do it. Not when I didn't want it.'

'Makes a bit of a change, doesn't it? So what happened?'

'She says I've been pinching tomatoes. My tomatoes.'

'Caught you at last, has she? Taken her long enough.'

He looked at her with jaundiced dislike.

'It explains something, then. Ana and me was wondering why she had that bloke along last Saturday afternoon.'

'What bloke?'

'Came from Mestara, so he said: acted queer enough. I asked him what he was seeing the señora about and all he did was wink and tap his nose. He did say, though, that he'd been working for a French señora in the Port who'd sold her place and was returning to France.'

'Working at what?'

'Gardening. Says he's grown the best tomatoes on the island.'

He leaned forward and picked the plastic bag out of the carrier. 'Take 'em.'

'We don't need any more.'

He emptied the tomatoes on to the drive and stamped them into pulp. He started the Mobylette, pushed it off its stand, sat on the saddle, and accelerated away. 'Sacked because of some bastard from Mestara,' he said furiously to an apricot tree as he rode past it.

Erington had been born in sight of the sea, in south Cornwall, and some of his earliest memories were of boats. He could remember how he had watched yachts set sail from the nearby harbour and how he had envied the owners and all who sailed in them because they were so fantastically rich. It was then that he had first learned that the eighth sin, poverty, is the most deadly of all.

He walked slowly down the narrow jetty, one of two built within the past few years in the harbour of Puerto Llueso to increase the number of berths, studying the craft which ranged from 11-foot dories to 30-foot sailing boats. He reached the end of the jetty and looked across the water at the western harbour arm against which were moored larger boats: a Bonetti motor yacht that had cost well over half a million pounds, three trawler yachts, several schooners built to face the seven seas . . . This was the world of the rich. And this was the world which he could now enter if only . . .

He turned round and saw Carol coming along the jetty. He suddenly remembered how, when he was just thirteen, he had gone with Stella to the woods at the back of the village and how she had been quite careless of the fact that he was held in contempt by almost all the other

children in the village because his mother was a slut and
his father had disappeared with the very toothy daughter
of a nearby landowner. He knew now the same sense of
excitement, expectation, and apprehension, as he had
known then.

'Hullo, Mark, I didn't expect to find you here.' Carol
was wearing a see-through blouse, under which was a
bikini top, jeans, and flip-flops. The light wind flicked
her hair into artfully sculptured shapes: the walk had
brought warm colour to her cheeks. 'Are you interested in
boats?'

'You sound surprised. Why shouldn't I be?' He smiled.
'On quick second thoughts, don't answer that.'

She liked the way in which he could mock himself. 'I
don't see much danger in answering. I'm surprised simply
and solely because you've never talked about them to me
and my experience is that anyone who's interested in
them can't keep off the subject for more than a few
minutes.'

'If I were lucky enough to own one, I'm sure I'd be in
there, talking.'

'What would you choose? That one?' She pointed across
the water to the Bonetti motor yacht.

He shook his head. 'She's for an owner who keeps a per-
manent crew to do all the work while he does all the
drinking . . . I'll take the ketch three berths along.'

'Really?'

'Why d'you say it like that?'

She shook her head, obviously embarrassed by her
question, put on the spur of the moment.

Hadn't she learned that appearances could be decep-
tive? he wondered, with a brief surge of resentment. He
might be dancing attendance on a rich middle-aged
woman, but that didn't mean he could only live with
luxury or that he would hesitate to fight a gale in a sound
ketch.

She swept a strand of hair away from her forehead.
' "If dreams were but the herald of reality." '

He laughed. 'Reality would be grossly overworked.'

'You dream a lot?'

'All the time, in glorious technicolour. But if you're
talking about real dreams, as opposed to day-dreams, I
usually end up in some ridiculous situation which probably means that subconsciously I've a fear of banana
skins.'

'Mark, do you always make fun of everything?'

'If I can . . .' He looked at his watch. 'I'm afraid I'd better get moving.'

'I'll come with you as far as the road.'

As they walked back along the jetty, he found himself
hoping that none of the people aboard the boats —
washing down, varnishing, merely letting the world move
on — would recognize them. Contemptuously, he cursed
himself for such weakness, forgetting how only minutes
before he had been assuring himself that he was not really
weak.

They reached the end of the jetty and walked between
two palm trees to enter the car park. The red Seat was
near by. He opened the driving door. If he asked her now
to go for a drive, he decided, she'd accept. Another
chance to be with her. But among the crowds of people in
the Port there must surely be more than one of the
juiceless English residents who would ask for nothing better than the chance to rush to Dolly to say she'd seen Mark
with a blonde. And there was no way that Dolly would
accept another blonde who'd thumbed a lift . . . 'Sorry
I've got to rush,' he said. He climbed into the car.

She looked at him with an expression he could not
read, then smiled goodbye and walked away. He started
the engine, backed, and drove out on to the front road,
turning left on to the Llueso road opposite the eastern
arm of the harbour.

There was not much traffic and soon he was free of the Port and driving along the straight, slowly rising road at 90. Rich men could always afford to follow their stars. If Dolly were to die now, he would be rich. Strangely, her murder didn't seem quite so ridiculously impossible now as it had before.

The sun beat down on his back as he lay face downwards on a towel by the pool. By his side was a glassful of Campari, sweet vermouth, and crushed ice.

What was it really like to kill someone? To know that one was playing at being God? Especially when the motive was gain not passion and therefore there could be no veil between the action and its effects.

As far as he knew, capital punishment was still legal in Spain even though it was some years now since such a sentence had been carried out. What was it like to wake up and know that this was one's last morning alive? To walk from one cell into another and to see (or to sense it, if one were blindfolded) the chair: to sit and to have the bonds secured: to feel the noose of the garrotte being adjusted over one's neck just before it was tightened . . . He felt the sweat break out. His imagination had always been much too vivid.

Yet that was to think in terms of failure. Think in terms of success. No one knew how many successful murders were committed in every country in every year because if they were successful the death was either never recorded or else recorded as accidental or natural. To murder successfully one needed to be clever, or lucky, or both. From the day he had left home he had been clever enough to know exactly what he wanted from life: he'd been lucky enough to get it.

He reached out to the glass, picked it up, and drank, his movements awkward because he couldn't be bothered to roll over and sit up. A clever man planned, but didn't believe that his cleverness must ensure success: he accepted that his plans might fail and therefore made allowances for failure. If Dolly's death appeared to be accidental, but through some mischance was identified as murder . . .

Dreaming, he thought bitterly: in glorious technicolour with both feet on a banana skin.

He lay in bed, staring up into the darkness, listening to the barking of a dog tied up in some field to 'guard' it.

It had been one hell of an evening. Dolly had returned from Palma in a temper because her hair hadn't been done exactly as she liked it. He'd made the mistake of try-ing to calm her down before he'd filled her up with alcohol. There'd been a row—although technically didn't it take two to have a row?—in which she'd reminded him that he owed her everything and if she chose to throw him out of the house he'd go naked because even the clothes he wore had been bought by her . . .

What was the safest way of faking an accident? If her death was identified as murder, how could he possibly escape suspicion when by her will he inherited everything? He had reached the stage of sleepiness where images floated through his mind in inconsequential sequence but still possessed some logic when a sudden thought jerked him fully awake. Dolly, in her desire for social standing, had turned her daughter's pathetic marriage into a happy and highly successful one. Why not use that lie to commit the perfect murder?

CHAPTER 9

Rockford walked into the post office and was surprised to find it empty. The man behind the counter checked through the mail, without first finding half a dozen other jobs to do, and handed him five letters. Less than thirty seconds from beginning to end, he estimated: if the staff weren't careful, they'd be in danger of deservedly getting a name for efficiency.

He went out into the street before checking through the letters, as he always did: service life had made him a man of habit, not that he ever allowed habit to become an end to itself. Four letters were for Cynthia. The fifth one was for him, from Garry. He slit open the envelope, took out the two typewritten pages, and read through them. When he'd finished he folded and replaced them in the envelope. He squared his shoulders. That was that. Torpedoed. But if the same sequence of events were to occur again, he would act exactly as he had before. A man's first duty was to his family: nothing could override that duty.

He walked through to the square and sat at one of the tables. He ordered a brandy and drank it, spoke to a couple of people he knew, continued through the village and along the winding lane and dirt track to Ca'n Bispo.

Cynthia was on the phone. Yes, of course they'd been invited to Dolly's party. But she really didn't know if they'd go. The evening was bound to be in the worst possible taste . . .

He took his pipe from his pocket and, very absent-mindedly, began to tap it out in the ashtray on an occasional table.

'Phillip!' she called out, one hand over the receiver.

'I've just spent hours cleaning everything.'

He picked up the ashtray, carried it through to the kitchen, and emptied it in the gash bucket. She couldn't see what he was doing, so he polished the ashtray with the bottom of his shirt. Back in the sitting-room, he replaced it exactly where it had been before.

Cynthia agreed over the phone that it was a pity so many of the new expatriates who had come to live in the area were NOCD, said goodbye, and replaced the receiver. 'That was Erato.'

Erato was the pencil-thin, middle-aged daughter of an aristocratic poetess. A bit of a mistake, he'd once called her: Cynthia had not been a-muse-d.

'She wanted to know if we were going to the party tonight. I said I wasn't certain.'

He remembered the dress she had carefully ironed earlier, her complaints as she ironed that she'd worn it so often people would recognize it before they recognized her, and her cold fury when she'd discovered that the clasp of the necklace of cultured pearls had broken.

'Was there any mail?' she asked.

'Four letters for you.'

'Might I have them, then?'

He took all the letters from his pocket: he passed the four unopened ones to her and kept the opened one in his right hand.

She sat in one of the armchairs and read. After a while, she looked up. 'Vera is coming to stay with us next month.'

Bad luck always seemed to sail in convoy, he thought.

'Phillip, did you hear what I said?'

'That's good,' he answered lamely.

'It means we simply have to have the spare bedroom redecorated: we can't possibly ask her to sleep in there with the walls all stained with that beastly damp mould. If only you'd done as I originally suggested . . .'

'Old girl, there's something I've got to say.'

She was astonished: she was unused to his interrupting her.

'This letter . . .' He held up his right hand. 'It's from Garry.'

'Then I hope it's to say he's paid the money into our bank account?'

'No.'

'Why hasn't he?'

'Because I'm afraid things didn't get better for him, they got worse. The business has gone for a burton.'

'It's what?' she said, almost whispering.

He went over to the window and looked out. It occurred to him that in moments of mental worry, the view of the land and the mountains somehow offered him quiet solace. 'As a matter of fact, the receiver's in.'

'What about our money?'

'Gone.'

'Don't be ridiculous. He's got to pay it back.'

'He can't. There's not even enough for the secured creditors.'

'D'you mean by that . . . You can't have lent him the money without security: you just can't.'

'He is my brother.'

'You're . . . you're senile.'

He took his pipe and began to rub the bowl against the palm of his left hand. 'I've been thinking . . . This place may not be a palace, but it is in the Huerta, with a bit of a garden and the telephone. People want to live here because it's rural, yet within easy walking distance of the village. It'll fetch a reasonable price. If we sell it . . .'

'What are you saying?'

'And buy a flat down in the Port, I think the difference would just be enough to invest and restore our income.'

'Live in a flat in the Port?' she said wonderingly.

'It's been on the cards for some time now, actually. You

see, with inflation roaring away as it has been, we've been living closer and closer to the line.'

'I am not moving to a flat in the Port.'

'I'm sure we'll be able to find one that's not too bad, especially if we can hang on until the winter and the prices ease.'

'I am not moving.'

His expression was sad. 'What I'm really trying to say, old fruit, is that we aren't going to have any option in the matter.'

Her face was strained. 'Don't you understand? I am not moving to a flat in the Port, as if I were some grocer's wife from Surbiton.'

If he were a grocer in Surbiton, he thought, they'd be moving from a flat into a villa. 'Then you'd prefer to go back home?'

'Go back?' She visualized the kind of life they would be forced to lead there in their greatly reduced circumstances.

'I'm sure we'll find somewhere nice in the Port . . .' He began. He stopped when he saw tears trickle down her cheeks. These were the first tears she had shed since the day his great friend and contemporary had gained promotion to flag rank and he had not. A man of compassion, he went to comfort her and put his hand on her shoulder. 'We'll get by. We've still each other which is the only thing that really matters.'

She jerked her shoulder free and then hysterically called him a failure and a fool.

As she entered Ca Na Nadana, each woman was presented with a corsage by Ana: delivered from Palma that late afternoon, each corsage was made up from two orchids.

Dolly received in the sitting-room. Her dress was unmistakably the very expensive product of a top couturier:

just as unmistakably, it did not suit a woman of her age at a private party in the heat of the summer. She also wore so much jewellery that each piece was devalued by all the others.

The garden was floodlit and the lighting had been installed by a retired electrical engineer who had worked in theatres. He was an artist. Colour had been used to melt shapes so that there was an infinity of space within which were shadowy recesses, each a small world on its own. Even the very large swimming pool had, with coloured underwater lights and prismatic reflectors, been turned into a shimmering rainbow.

There was, of course, champagne to drink. But those without an educated palate were able to ask for whatever other drink they preferred. Smoked salmon and pâté-de-foie-gras appetizers were served initially with the drinks.

A barbecue, set beyond two weeping pear trees, had been fashioned as a grotto and this was watched over by two hobgoblins. The chef, who normally worked in a restaurant in the Port and was in full uniform, cooked kebabs to order: guests could choose whatever combination they wanted from various meats, pineapple, and giant prawns. To the right of the grotto was a rose bower in which were served five different kinds of local sponge cakes, fruit salad and cream, ice-cream, rum babas, chocolate éclairs, and meringues. There was a very wide choice of liqueurs, ranging from cognac to Tia Maria.

'Never in the field of social conflict,' said one of the guests, after his sixth glass of champagne, 'was so much offered by so few to so many.'

Had Erington been there, he would almost certainly have managed to prevent Dolly making quite such a fool of herself: he would have persuaded her not to drink so much, so quickly, and when she tried to boast he would tactfully have guided the conversation to fresh subjects.

But he was in England, called there by a telegram from his younger brother which had told him that his mother was very seriously ill and calling for him. Dolly had demanded he get his priorities right and stay for the party, but he had insisted on leaving immediately, defying both her tears and her threats.

By nine-forty-five, as night drifted in on a stillness so complete that not a leaf stirred, Dolly had drunk enough champagne to forget any need to dissemble her feelings. 'I had heard John and Patty were in some sort of financial mess, yes. But, of course, really that's been obvious for a long time: that terrible old car which looks just like a wreck and those pathetic parties. And even going around trying to do odd jobs to make a few pesetas. As I've always said, people shouldn't be allowed to come out here unless they can afford to live decently. Apart from any other reason, it's up to us to set a standard.'

'Set a standard for whom?'

She frowned slightly as she tried to focus her gaze and discover who, among the several people grouped loosely around her, had spoken. She noticed the look of super-cilious disdain on Kim Covert's face. 'A standard for the locals, of course.' She despised the Coverts. They were from an old county family who had lost their money, yet had never learned to hold their heads lower.

'You think they would want to follow the standards some of the wealthier foreigners set?'

Covert's wife said in a low voice: 'Shut up, Kim.'

He refused to shut up. 'On the principle, no doubt, of the shipwrecked seaman who finally reaches shore and sees a gibbet and says, "Thank God, civilization."?'

'I don't know what on earth you're talking about: ship-wrecks, gibbets.'

Victoriana walked into the middle of the group and held out the large silver salver on which were more than a dozen full glasses of champagne. Most of those present refused any more, but Dolly reached out and put down her empty glass with too much force. Victoriana was momentarily unable to keep the salver level and champagne spilled over the rims of some of the glasses. Dolly upbraided her for carelessness, picked up a glass, and drank eagerly. Covert, using unnecessary care, put his glass down on the tray. He picked up a full glass and thanked Victoriana with grave courtesy. He raised his glass. 'I drink to all those who, by their actions, set such pointed examples for the locals.'

His wife said, now really angry: 'If you go on like this, I'll kill you.'

Dolly, between mouthfuls of champagne, returned to the subject they had previously been discussing. 'I just can't think how people can come out here when they can't afford to live reasonably. Haven't they any pride?'

'Are you criticizing them for lack of pride or lack of money?' Covert was nearly as drunk as Dolly, but this fact was obvious only to those who knew that when sober he was invariably, if at times chillingly, polite.

'Both.'

'So to be proudly honest but poor is not qualification enough: to be proudly dishonest and rich is?'

'There's no need for anyone to be poor.'

'No? Have you, then, discovered some secret which we lesser — and poorer — mortals have been denied?'

It finally occurred to Dolly that he was being rude. 'It's easy enough making money playing the markets,' she answered, laughing to herself because Covert's father had lost the family fortune on the stockmarket.

'Markets in what? Scrap iron?'

She did not know that her late husband was popularly supposed to have made his money as a scrap iron merchant. 'Scrap iron? . . . Buying and selling shares and commodities, of course.'

'I've always understood that that's very tricky? For in-

stance, I don't suppose that you have ever actually
managed to make a genuine profit doing that, have you?'
    She drained her glass. 'I've made as much as anyone.'
    'Really?'
    'I made over forty thousand pounds seven months ago.
How about that?'
    'I think I'd describe that as unbelievable.'
    'I knew gold was going to go up, so I bought when the
price was under five hundred and sold at over six hundred. Forty thousand pounds and not a penny in tax. And
d'you know what I did with the forty thousand?'
    'Invested it in Striker and Cabbot?'
    If he'd hoped to confuse her, he failed. 'A firm about to
go bankrupt?' She tapped the largest and most ostentatious piece of jewellery she was wearing, a brooch made
from a solitaire diamond set around with rubies. 'I
bought this.'
    'That really cost you forty thousand pounds? I am sur-
prised. I'd no idea inflation had become so bad that
costume jewellery was that expensive.'
    It was a cheap, obvious remark and therefore untypical
of him. His wife took his arm and, digging her nails into
his bare flesh—he wore a short-sleeved linen shirt with a
silk neckerchief—forced him to walk away. In a low voice
she told him what she thought of his behaviour in terms
normally restricted by the county to the hunting field and
croquet.

CHAPTER 10

Alvarez awoke. He stared up at the pattern on the ceiling,
formed by the light coming up through the shutters and a
gap in the curtains, and knew he had some reason for
feeling contented. Then he remembered. Today was Sun-

day and he did not have to go to the office.

He was about to drift off to sleep again when his head began to ache and he awoke fully, first because of his sense of irritation, then because of the discomfort . . . He remembered how, when he and Jaime had insisted on finishing the bottle of brandy the previous night, Dolores had called them a couple of drunken Andalucian gypsies . . . Thank God he could stay in bed all morning . . .

Downstairs, the telephone rang.

It couldn't be for him, he assured himself: not on a Sunday, not when he was rapidly beginning to feel that death could be only a merciful release.

He heard Dolores shout at Jaime and Jaime shout at Dolores. Jaime, he thought with brief, perverse satisfaction would be feeling even worse than he: Jaime always did.

The telephone was finally answered. Let it not be for me, he thought, and I promise on my sacred honour . . .

'Enrique,' Dolores shouted.

He pulled himself into a sitting position and the room shivered and his stomach churned. Never again would he touch another drop of brandy . . .

'Are you ever coming down?'

He slowly swivelled round and stood. He put on a thin dressing-gown over his pyjama trousers, left the bedroom, and tottered downstairs.

Dolores, her jet black hair glistening from prolonged brushing and swept back against the sides of her head and tied into a bun, brilliant brown eyes as freshly bright as a midsummer dawn, studied him. She put her hands on her hips. 'You look terrible!'

He felt terrible. Yet not many minutes before he had woken up and momentarily revelled in life. He tottered over to the phone. 'Yes?' he croaked.

'Took you long enough,' said the guard who was telephoning from the guardia post.

'D'you expect me to break my neck rushing?'

'You'll never break your neck, mate: just drown it.'

'All right, cut out the smart cracks. What's the panic that's got you interrupting my day off?'

'Some rich foreign woman's popped it up in the Huerta.'

'So?'

'So the doc who's been called said to tell you.'

'Why?'

'How would I know that?'

'Where's she live?'

'Ca Na Nadana. It's off the road leading up to Festona Valley.'

'What's her name?'

'I did hear it, but all these foreign names sound like you're clearing your throat . . . Have fun!' He laughed, rang off.'

Alvarez walked slowly into the kitchen.

Dolores studied him once more. 'I told you not to keep on drinking. I said you'd regret it this morning. Have you looked in a mirror?'

'No more, please. If you've an ounce of pity, make me a cup of coffee.'

'Ha! Last night I was a damn fool woman who kept try-ing to spoil a man's fun. This morning, however, it's please be kind to me . . . Why should we women be kind to you men who are all such selfish fools? Did I give you the headache? Did I say, have another drink and then another? Did I insist on trying to tell the whole world that the mayor of Llueso, the Governor of the Baleares, and the Prime Minister of Spain, all should be sacked because none of them know about running the country?'

He sighed, turned, went back upstairs. It wasn't the women who needed liberating, it was the men.

Alverez slowed the car as he reached a T-junction and in front of him, nailed to a convenient telegraph pole, were half a dozen name boards shaped to show in which direction the houses lay. Ca Na Nadana was to the left, along the dirt track.

He drove slowly because the surface was poor and his car was old, but even so the suspension thumped badly. Already the heat was sufficient to turn the interior of the car into a Turkish bath and as he bounced up and down, to the accompaniment of stabbing pains in his head, the sweat broke out on his face, neck, back, and chest. Sunday, bloody Sunday!

The dirt track divided at a T-junction, but the way ahead was overgrown with weeds. He turned right. The first house on the left was large and set behind elaborate entrance gates, but as he slowed he saw a nameplate: Ca Na Yelta. He drove on and the next house became visible over a belt of cypress. The entrance to this house proved to be far more elaborate than the previous one and a carved namestone, looking to his jaundiced eyes very like a gravestone, told him that this indeed was Ca Na Nadana.

He entered the drive and as he braked to a halt he stared with some amazement at the lawn which on the south side curled right round to the drive: how ever many thousands of litres of water a day did it take to keep the grass that green? Easy to judge that the owner of this place had no conception of the value of money.

He parked to the side of the front door, left the car, crossed the drive, and rang the bell. He heard a dog begin to yap. Then the door was opened by Victoriana and he introduced himself before stepping inside. A remarkably ill-proportioned small dog stared at him with bulging eyes and continued to yap until Victoriana shouted at it to shut up. 'There's no other car here—has the doc gone?' he asked.

'He left some time ago because he said he couldn't wait any longer. Said he'd come back as soon as he could.' She tried to be her usual boisterously confident self, but could not hide the effect of the shock she had received. 'He said to give you the key.'

'What key?'

'Of the bedroom, of course.' She studied him more closely. 'You look kind of a bit worn out.'

'I feel completely worn out, señorita. I was working very late last night.'

'Then first of all d'you feel like something to wake you up? Coffee and a coñac?'

He hesitated.

'Let's go through to the kitchen and I'll get it for you.'

The kitchen was the most luxuriously appointed one he had ever seen. Tiled from floor to ceiling, with matching cupboards and working surfaces, on which were stacked a large number of glasses and plates, there was a split-level electric cooker, with ceramic hob, a gas cooker, a very large refrigerator and a walk-in deepfreeze, washing-up machine, and enough further equipment to start a shop. In one corner there was an eating area and she told him to sit there while she prepared things. He watched her fill an electric coffee-maker and switch it on.

'I'll get the coñac. Carlos One do you?'

'There's no need for anything like that,' he said, without conviction.

'We never drink anything else.'

He settled back against the padded wooden shoulder rest. Victoriana went over to one of the cupboards and brought out a bottle with a Soberano label. 'Don't go by what it says.' She winked as she handed him the bottle. 'What the eye don't see, the heart don't grieve about.' The fact that she was no longer alone had cheered her up and much of her pert manner had returned. She went to another cupboard for a glass.

As he poured out a large brandy, he said: 'So who works here apart from you?'

'There's Ana—she's at home because it's her day off. And old Angel. No. I keep forgetting, he's gone and that new bloke's with us.'

'New bloke?'

'Galmes: Miguel Galmes: comes from Mestara. Only you don't need to be told that, not with him so rude and surly.' The people from Mestara, only six kilometres away, had always been disliked by the people from Llueso: no one really knew why.

'What's he do?'

'Works in the garden. Says he's twice the gardener old Angel was, but if you ask me that's all talk.'

'And who's Angel?'

'Angel Matas.'

'He died?'

'Not him: got careless.'

'How d'you mean, señorita?'

'I shouldn't have said that.' She looked uneasily at him. 'My mum always says I speak much more'n I think.' She shook her head. 'But going upstairs with the señora's tea and finding her dead . . .' She shivered. She got a glass for herself and poured out a brandy.

'Why did Angel give up gardening here?' he asked patiently.

She sat on the opposite side of the table. 'It wasn't really fair, was it? I mean, he had grown the tomatoes.'

'Señorita, you will have to explain.'

She drank. 'He can be an awkward squad, no question. As cunning as a cartload of monkeys. Know how he used to get her to give him a rise in wages?' She explained how Matas had deliberately done something that would annoy the señora so that she'd sack him and how, before he left the job, he'd fix the automatic watering system so that it wouldn't work. She and Ana had always known what he'd done, of course, but they weren't going to split on him and the señor never put himself out to discover how to overcome the trouble . . .

'The señor?'

'Señor Erington.'

'He lives here?'

The coffee-machine began to hiss. She finished her brandy, crossed to the machine and switched it off. 'How d'you like it—black or white?'

'Black,' he answered immediately.

She poured the coffee into two mugs, set these on the table, brought a silver sugar bowl from a cupboard and a silver cream jug from the refrigerator. Absentmindedly, he helped himself to a second brandy. 'Who is this señor?'

Señor Erington, she answered, had lived in the house for quite a long time now. He was, of course, very much younger than the señora . . . She looked at Alvarez out of the corner of her eyes.

The English were strange people, he thought. Where was their pride? A woman with all the money that the señora so obviously had, buying herself a man perhaps half her age: and a man who was content to prostitute himself to a middle-aged widow when the world was filled with beautiful young women eager to be stormed and conquered . . . 'When did he go to England?'

'It was two days before the party, so it must've been Thursday. You ought to have heard the señora! Telling him he musn't go until after the party and that his mother would have to wait to see him even if she was dying.'

This really shocked Alvarez.

'She started shouting that if he went she wouldn't have him back in the house. I thought that'd stop him: he likes the rich life too much. But it didn't. He told her straight, it didn't matter what she did, he was going to England to see his mother.'

He nodded approvingly. A gigolo, but a gigolo with some backbone left.

She finished her brandy and stirred two spoonfuls of

sugar into her coffee. 'When she couldn't get him to stay with threats, she tried crying. What a sight that was! . . . Holy mother!' she said suddenly. 'The señora is dead and here am I talking like this.'

Alvarez made no comment, correctly if cynically believing Victoriana's sudden expression of conscience owed more to effect than to conviction. 'What was the party all about?'

Victoriana said slyly: 'I think she gave her parties just to show how rich she was. You ought to see the dress she bought specially—it's hanging up in one of the cupboards. Know what it cost? Over a hundred thousand pesetas.'

'Impossible,' he said immediately.

'She told me so herself: over a hundred thousand pesetas.'

Even today, that money would buy somewhere between five hundred and a thousand square metres of good land. How could anyone begin to spend so much land on a frock?

'And the jewels! She once told me they were insured for over twenty million!'

She was clearly capable of any stupidity. 'I'd better have a look at her.' He stood and immediately his head began to pound once more.

'D'you want me . . . Like, to come with you?'

'Just to show me which is the room, that's all.'

She was very relieved to learn she would not have to go into the bedroom. She led the way into the hall, where Lulu met them, and up the stairs to the first floor.

'Does the señora have a family?' he asked.

'She's a daughter back in England. Very rich with a husband who makes millions of pesetas a year.'

Wealth, he thought, bred wealth: just as poverty bred poverty.

They went along a wide corridor to a door panelled in a

dark, finely grained wood. 'That's her bedroom . . . When I went in first of all, I thought she was just still asleep. But I opened the shutters and saw her face . . .' She became silent.

'Señorita, it will have been a terrible shock for you. Go back downstairs now and try to forget what you saw in there.' He waited until she had returned to the head of the stairs, then put the key in the lock and opened the door.

The shutters of one of the three windows had been clipped back and the curtain drawn, and sharp sunlight was streaming in. The room was over furnished with pieces which even to his unknowing eyes were obviously of exceptional quality. He noticed a small pile of underclothes, carefully folded on the needleworked seat of one of a set of two walnut armchairs, a framed photograph of a woman in her early twenties on the bow-fronted dressing-table, and to the right of this a large, finely grained leather jewel case.

He approached the bed. He had seen death too often to be afraid of it, yet had never lost his awe of its presence, or his reverence for the dead. He believed that after death each man and woman faced judgement and therefore was to be pitied, because who could avoid doing wrong? But he also believed that when such wrongs had not been designed deliberately to hurt others then such judgement was always merciful.

She lay on her back, face pointing directly up to the ceiling. Her eyes were closed and her mouth was slightly twisted to the right with lips parted. Her flesh had sagged and, although he was not to know this, in death she at last looked her age. At some time before her death she had vomited.

There was a satin quilted headboard which at each end had a bedside table with drawers: on the right-hand one was a medicine bottle, together with a small empty cardboard container and a printed pamphlet, still folded. He tried to read the label on the bottle, but the small print defeated his eyesight and he had forgotten to bring his glasses—glasses were an acknowledgement of advancing age which he was not yet prepared to make.

He straightened up, crossed to the two shuttered windows, and opened the shutters. Both windows faced west and he could see the mountains which marked the head of the Laraix valley. Gaunt, grey rock, pock-marked with the greens and browns of weed grasses, wild bushes, and occasional pine trees, speared upwards into the bitingly brilliant blue sky. He looked down at the garden. Here and there he could see bits of paper lying about on the lawn and he guessed that a bright point of light marked a glass, either broken or merely discarded. But as he continued to stare down he noticed that near the drystone wall on the north side of the garden the grass had begun to lose colour in a pattern. It was quite some time before he realized that if the pattern were continued in places where it faltered, the word 'Putta'—whore—was spelled out.

CHAPTER 11

Dr Rosselló was small, even by Mallorquin standards, with a body just beginning to put on weight. Seen full on his face was round, seen in profile it was triangular with the end of his nose a very sharp apex: he had a small, pepper-and-salt coloured moustache over a straight mouth. His expression made it fairly obvious that he was a man who seldom had found cause to doubt his own infallibility.

He spoke to Alvarez in the sitting-room. 'I waited here as long as I could, but I then had to leave with a couple of patients to visit.' His tone was critical.

Alvarez forbade to point out that he, in his turn, had had to wait quite a long time for the doctor.

'You'll have been up and had a look at her—did you notice anything?'

'Nothing unusual.'

'Ha!' He was a good doctor, but a pompous man. He cupped his hands behind his back and paced the length of the sitting-room: Lulu on the settee, bewildered by the absence of people she knew, watched him with bulging eyes and at infrequent intervals gave a short yap which patently annoyed him. 'You are no doubt aware that there was a party here last night? Clearly the señora drank a great deal. In fact, she was constantly doing so and then calling for me the next day on the pretext that she was suffering from some complaint.' He sniffed his disapproval.

Over the past few minutes, Alvarez's headache had increased in strength. Initially he had thought he might consult the doctor on what would bring the quickest relief: now, he decided against asking.

'She had another regrettable habit. She was constantly taking sleeping pills. Quite unnecessary if one lives a healthy life. The two habits if indulged in together can have a fatal effect. I warned her several times against taking sleeping pills after drinking alcohol on the grounds that alcohol has a recognized adjuvant effect. Do you understand what that means?'

'It increases the effect of the pills?'

Rosselló looked irritated, disliking, as an expert, a layman's simplification. 'Alcohol substantially reduces the minimum lethal dose. In respect of the drug the señora took, the fatal dose would normally be somewhere between fifteen and twenty-five tablets: after a large intake of alcohol the lethal dose would be as low as five.' He stopped pacing the floor by the French windows, turned, and stared at Alvarez. When there was no comment, he continued speaking. 'Almost all proprietary pills these days contain very carefully calculated amounts of antagonists to combat the accidental taking of a fatal dose: the situation where someone takes his or her regular dose; falls asleep, half wakes up and thereupon thinks he or she has failed to take it and swallows another full dose. The pills the señora took contain the antagonistic ITC, which is a purgative. Other proprietary pills contain substances such as ipecacuanha, an emetic as well as a purgative: since vomiting can be highly dangerous when a person is not fully conscious, the use of emetics is becoming much less.'

'She had vomited,' said Alvarez.

'Quite so!' replied Rossello with satisfaction. 'Which is one of the reasons why you are here.'

'But assuming she drank too much, surely that could explain . . .'

He held up a hand. 'Please allow me to finish. There was by the bedside—you may have noticed it . . .' There was a doubtful note in his voice. 'A bottle which contained sleeping pills, the small cardboard container in which the bottle is sold, and the instructions pamphlet which accompanies it. Would you agree that the presence of the last two items suggests that the bottle was a new one, opened during the night?'

Alvarez nodded.

'I counted the number of pills remaining and there were thirty-one. The bottle originally held fifty. Nineteen pills if taken together with a large amount of alcohol form without question a lethal dose. Yet nineteen pills contain sufficient ITC to ensure a somewhat violent reaction.' He paused, then said crisply: 'There was no such reaction.'

Alvarez, unable to remain standing any longer, sat on the settee. Lulu moved across and nuzzled his hand and he fondled her ears. Rosselló was looking intently at him, obviously expecting some comment, so he said: 'The rest of the pills must have fallen to the floor and rolled under the bed. I mean, if she was really tight when she took them . . .'

'Quite. But that lies within your province, not mine.'

'Of course, she might have opened the bottle a couple of days before and the cardboard case and instructions were just left lying around . . .'

'That also is within your province,' Rosselló ran the palm of his right hand over his sleek hair. 'Because of the questions raised by the missing pills, I examined the body of the señora with even more than my normal extreme care. During this examination I observed, on brow and face, what may be Tardieu spots, or petechiæ. Do you understand their significance?'

Alvarez was certain he should do, but his thumping brain refused to recall the answer.

'They are invariably a sign of asphyxiation.'

'You . . . you're telling me she was murdered?'

'I am informing you of the fact that the possibility exists: it will require a post mortem to confirm or deny such possibility. However, if you press me for an immediate conclusion, I give my opinion that this is a case of murder. And here it is necessary to remember that asphyxiation often induces terminal vomiting.

'Naturally, I ascertained the time of death: I would put this as having taken place at four a.m. . . . . I must remind you that such an estimate can never be accepted as accurate because of the many varied and often contradictory, even unascertainable, surrounding factors.' He sounded annoyed by this breach in the armour of his certainty. 'Well, I must leave and continue with my work.' He walked with sharp, abrupt movements over to the door.

'Can you hang on a sec?' Alvarez unwillingly came to his feet. 'There's one thing I can't really understand. If

she was asphyxiated, why are nineteen sleeping pills missing—assuming they aren't on the floor?'

Rosselló said: 'Clearly, the question and answer both lie
within your province, not mine.' He continued to the
doorway and went out into the hall.

A great man for provinces, thought Alvarez. He heard
the front door shut, a car engine start up, and then the
crunch of tyres on the stone chip surface of the drive.

He slowly made his way to the kitchen and slumped
down on one of the bench seats in the eating area.

Victoriana, who was stacking dirty glasses and crockery
in the dishwasher, straightened up and studied him. 'You
look worse than ever.'

'I feel even worse than that.'

'You ought to have asked the doc for something to
help.'

'He only hands out long lectures.'

'You can say that again! Went on and on at me over
those sleeping pills. Wasn't my fault, was it? If the señora
swallowed half a bottle, what was it to do with me?'

'You should have told him it wasn't your province . . .
Come and sit down. I want to ask you something.'

When she was seated opposite him, he said: 'Tell me,
who slept here last night?'

'Me and the señora.'

'Not Ana?'

'She went off as soon as we'd cleared up as much as we
were going to. She lives in the village and when it's her
day off she always spends the night before and the night
after at home.'

'What did you do after she left?'

'Went to bed, of course. After spending all day on my
feet, working for the señora, d'you think I was going to
rush off to a disco?'

'Did you turn in before she did?'

'No way! She couldn't get to bed quickly enough the

moment the last guest left. Talk about tight! Didn't think
she was going to get up the stairs.'

'I suppose you got her room ready for her to turn in?'

'Had to do that half way through the party when
people weren't boozing so much and there was just
enough time to nip up and turn the bed down.'

'Did you happen to notice if the bottle of pills, the case
it came in, and the instructions pamphlet, were by the
side of the bed?'

'There wasn't nothing there. I always check to make
certain everything's neat and tidy. That's a job on its own
with the way she leaves everything lying around.'

'Where did she normally keep her sleeping pills?'

'In one of the cabinets in the bathroom. Like a
chemist's shop. She was always taking so many pills it's a
wonder she didn't rattle when she walked.'

'Have you any idea of how many bottles of sleeping pills
are in the cabinet?'

'Wouldn't know.'

'If she went to bed right away, I suppose you did the
shutting up of the house?'

'Like always, after a party.'

'How d'you go about it? Tell me the sequence.'

'I just did it—there weren't no sequence. Locked the
doors, made certain all the shutters were fast. The air-
conditioning had been switched off in the sitting-room
because of the people having to pass through and the outside doors being opened, so there was no need to close
that down for the night.'

'Could you possibly have left a door or a shutter open
by mistake?'

'No way.'

'Did you open up this morning before you went into her
bedroom?'

'Always do, at eight sharp. Not that either of 'em is ever
down then.'

'Were any of the doors or shutters open?'

' 'Course they weren't . . .' Rather belatedly, she realized the implications of his questions. 'Here, you're not saying someone broke into this place last night?'

'I don't know yet.'

'But . . . but . . .'

'Whereabouts do you sleep, señorita?'

'At the back.'

'Do you hear much of what goes on in the rest of the house?'

'Not really—not unless there's a lot of noise like the señor playing music very loud.'

'Did you hear anything during the night?'

She thought back. 'Only her.' She pointed at Lulu, who had waddled into the kitchen and climbed into the dog basket under the central table. 'Had a bit of a bark, which kind of woke me, but not all the way, if you know what I mean?'

He smiled. 'You came up to the surface but very soon went deep down again?'

'That's about it.'

'Any idea of what time that was?'

'Not really, no.'

'There's a photo up in the bedroom of a young woman—is that her daughter?'

'That's right. Looks quite nice now, doesn't she? D'you reckon she'll get this house?'

'I'd think so, yes.'

'Wonder if she'll want me and Ana to stay on.'

If she didn't, he thought, neither of the two should have much trouble in finding another job. The señora had obviously demanded a high standard of work: these days, despite the high rate of unemployment, there were always positions for well trained staff. 'Have you any idea who was her solicitor?'

'She usually went to a bloke in Palma: don't know his

name but his office was somewhere close to Jaime Three. But she did recently go to Señor Vives, here in the village.'

'I don't suppose you know why she suddenly went to a local solicitor?'

'Of course not,' she said virtuously.

He thought for a moment. 'Whereabouts in this place does she keep her personal papers?'

'Depends what you mean by personal papers. She kept things in the study and didn't like anyone else going in there unless it was to give a quick dust round. And then she kept a good eye open to see what was happening. Could be in there, couldn't they?'

'It certainly sounds likely. Which room is the study?'

'The one on the right of the hall as you come into the house.'

'I'd better have a look in there . . . You've been a great help. Thanks.'

She showed signs of fresh uneasiness. 'What's going to happen? I mean, are you staying on here?'

'Certainly for a little while.'

'You . . . Does that mean . . . Didn't she just die?'

'I don't know one way or the other right now.'

'But maybe . . . she was killed?'

'It's possible.'

She shivered. She looked up at the electric clock on the wall. 'It's coming up to lunch . . . Wouldn't like to stop and have some grub here, would you? She'd said she wanted gambas, steak, and chocolate mousse, and it's all ready. Seems a pity not to use the food up, doesn't it?'

To some extent Victoriana had remained insulated from the death of the señora when it had seemed to be due to natural causes. But now it was possible that the señora might have been murdered, she was scared to be in the house on her own. Clearly, it would be a kindness to stay with her for as long as was possible. The fact that grilled gambas was his favourite dish did not, he assured himself, in any way influence his decision to remain.

The three men from the undertakers were quiet, efficient, and quick. They wrapped the body in a modified flexible stretcher and carried it out to the Seat 124 which had a vanlike body and was painted black.

Alvarez watched them drive out on to the dirt track, then returned into the house. He must remember to phone Superior Chief Salas tomorrow morning and tell that great man what had happened. He thought gloomily that Salas, in his imperious Madrileño manner, would inevitably find fault in whatever had been done.

He turned and entered the study, examined the bookcases, the small cupboard, the filing cabinet, and finally the desk. The long drawer and the top drawer on the left of the kneehole were locked and it seemed reasonable to assume that it was in one or other of these that she kept her confidential papers. He checked everywhere a second time, looking for the keys, but failed to find them. Perhaps Victoriana would know where they were kept.

She was sunbathing by the swimming pool, wearing a brief bikini. She seemed to have lost her earlier sense of apprehension and, not for the first time, he envied the young their ability to switch emotions so quickly. 'Señorita, I have been looking around in the study and find the desk is locked. Have you any idea where the keys to this are?'

She shook her head. There was a patio chair nearby and he sat. She continued to look at him for a while, then settled, her head pillowed on her outstretched arms, her back burning hot from the sun. He thought about the keys. If Victoriana had no idea where they were kept, then clearly they would not be found in any of the places which a maid might clean or otherwise investigate. That surely left the señora's handbags or, if she didn't want to carry the keys around with her, an unusual hiding-place. He closed his eyes, the better to identify all possible hiding-places.

When he awoke, Victoriana had gone and, as he discovered, so had his headache. He went indoors and upstairs to the master bedroom and there, twenty minutes later, he found two small keys on a key ring in the toe of a shoe, one of dozens on the racks in the bottom of the built-in cupboards.

One key opened the top, long drawer of the kneehole desk in the study. The jumble of papers inside was daunting, but on the top was a large brown envelope and inside this he found two copies of the señora's will, one in Spanish, the other in English. He read the Spanish copy. Everything she owned was left to Mark Erington with the sole exception of a pewter cigarette case which was to go to George Trent.

Why had Trent been left what was clearly a very ordinary cigarette case? A sentimental gift? But if she had had a gram of sentiment in her, she would surely have left at least part of her fortune to her daughter? . . . The feeling within him grew that there was some special significance to be attached to the terms of this will, but for the life of him he couldn't imagine what that could be.

CHAPTER 12

Kenley walked up to the hedge and carefully trimmed one corner of it.

Lettie spoke wearily. 'Come back here, Steve.'

He stared beyond the hedge at the road where their car was parked and there was a look of yearning on his face.

'It's no good your running away. We've got to talk this matter out.'

He turned. There was a sudden catch in his throat when he first saw the plaster on her leg, as there always was, even after all these months, even though he had last seen it not very long before. Slowly he walked back across the garden.

'Sit down.'

He sat in the second patio chair, set just within the shade of the house.

'She's dead,' said Lettie.

He nodded. At first he had thought that the report of Dolly's death must be just one more rumour, but earlier he had met a friend who had assured him it was true.

'And all she has referring to the loan is your signed statement agreeing the total amount borrowed? There was nothing in writing about interest?'

'No.'

'Then no one can demand any interest from you.'

'But if she thought I'd given my word . . .'

'Stop being so soft.' She saw his hurt look and put out her hand to rest it on his. 'I didn't mean to be nasty, but you've just got to be realistic.'

He said nothing.

'And anyway, it'll be her daughter who gets the estate and she won't try to charge twenty per cent.'

He wondered. A chip off the old block could very accurately describe some family relationships.

'She won't even know about the twenty per cent . . . if you don't tell her.'

That was true. Unless Dolly had made a note of the final agreement. Not that that would have any legal validity. But then there never had been any legal validity . . .

'You know exactly what you meant and that's what you'll stick to. How can you possibly be more honest to yourself than that?'

He turned to look at her and saw all the determination

in the tight line of her mouth. Her conviction convinced him. She had to be right. Never mind what false assumptions Dolly had made . . . Yet he was no sooner certain than he began once more to doubt. An honourable man surely didn't let subsequent circumstances alter his position? If Dolly really had believed . . .

She could judge how his thoughts were running. She said, her voice hard: 'I'm sorry, but now she's dead you just aren't going to do any more than pay back the capital, less what you've already given her, to her executors.'

He wished he could see everything as clearly as she did. But he could feel himself once more giving in to her and he was grateful to her for being so strong that he was certain that this time his surrender could be made with honour.

'I suppose you've heard?' said Carol, as she put her towel down on the hot sand.

'Heard what?' asked Trent, as he pulled off his shirt.

'About Dolly.'

'What's the old bag been up to now?'

'She died last night.'

He undid his shorts and stepped out of them: he was wearing a pair of multi-coloured swimming trunks. 'She's actually done the decent thing for once?'

'I don't like people saying things like that.'

He shrugged his shoulders, sat on his towel. He reached across to his shorts and brought out a pack of cigarettes and a lighter.

'Why d'you hate her so?' she asked, as she settled on the towel. 'She couldn't help being the kind of person she was.'

'Stop believing in the old-fashioned kind of fairies.'

She stared at him, the sunshine cutting across her face. 'What does that mean exactly?'

'It means it's time you scrapped your rose-tinted spectacles. Dolly was a bitch.'

'I know she was a bit of a snob, but some snobs are really quite nice people if you bother to get to know them.'

'In your book, Dracula was quite a nice person once one became used to his odd drinking habits.'

'I hate looking for the worst in people.'

'You can be so blind you don't see it even when you come face to face with it.'

'Maybe that's why I think you're quite a nice person, even when you're in a foul mood?' She took off her clothes to reveal a bikini. She sat with her legs raised and her hands clasped in front of them. There was something about his dislike of Dolly which she didn't understand and which frightened her.

A power boat, a hundred metres off shore, had been waiting for a water skier to give the OK signal. Suddenly the engine accelerated with a bellow of sound and the bows knifed through the water, bringing the skier to a standing position. For a brief moment it looked as if he might lose his balance, then he regained it to flash across the water at thirty knots.

'I wonder what Dolly's daughter's like?' she said.

'Quite a nice person, really.'

She laughed. At least he hadn't lost his sense of humour.

Matas sat on a chair in the road immediately outside his front door and smoked a pipe. He saw his daughter, Rosa, walking towards him with her current boy-friend and he watched the young man with very sharp eyes to make certain there was no undue familiarity. When they reached him, the young man said good evening, then they both went inside to watch television. That was all right. His wife would make certain there was no hanky-panky.

Life had changed all right, but not always for the better. When he'd been young, there'd been no chance of respectable daughters getting into trouble, but these days they'd been given so much freedom that there was every chance. But Rosa wasn't going to end up with a little bastard.

Two men, of roughly his age, one of them using a stick because he still suffered from the leg he had broken months before when working on a house, walked up the road. They stopped by his chair, but for a while said nothing as they allowed time to wash slowly over them. Finally, the elder of the two said: 'What's the name of the foreign señora you used to work for?'

He took the pipe from his mouth. 'Señora Lund.' He hawked and spat.

'I thought that was it. She's dead.'

Matas returned the pipe to his mouth and smoked.

'Found cold in bed this morning.'

He thought about the tomatoes and knew a fresh surge of anger that she should have sacked him for taking his own tomatoes.

'Been ill, has she?'

'Only when she's been on the booze,' he answered contemptuously.

'Did she have a party there last night?'

'I wasn't there, was I, so I can't say.'

'Old Juan says there was.'

'Then you know more'n I do.' There'd been a row after each one of her previous parties. She'd wanted him to return the next day to clean up the garden and he'd stubbornly refused to work on a Sunday.

'There ain't no funeral tonight.'

He finally, if briefly, showed some surprise. 'No funeral?'

'They say as the doc called in the police.'

There was a silence, broken by the passing of a couple

of badly silenced motor-bikes, then by the elder of the two. 'Feel like a glass?'

Matas stood. He picked up the chair and put it just inside the house. They walked slowly up the road, careful to stay on the shadowed side because the sun was still very hot.

There was something about the air around Llueso which prompted infidelity, not just among the young but also among couples who had been married long enough for an observer to imagine that they would have come to prefer marital routine to marital rapine. James Wraight and Penelope Marston had been happily married when they arrived on the island, though not to each other: soon after meeting they deserted their respective spouses and lived together in a flat in Puerto Llueso where they had tremendous fun giving parties at which everyone drank too much. There was no social stigma attached to behaviour such as theirs: only if they had also been rather poor would they have been ostracized.

Their sitting-room was packed with people and although doors and windows were open and two fans were running at fast speed, the air was thick with smoke and stiflingly hot.

Rockford edged his way inside. He waved hullo to Penelope over the heads of some arguing, sweating people, and was handed a glass by Wraight who didn't bother to find out what he would like.

'Where's Cynthia?' asked Wraight, shouting to make himself heard.

'Got a bit of a head,' he shouted back. 'Sends all her apologies.'

'Of course she's got a bit of a head,' said Pam, a blonde standing next to him. She liked him and could never understand why he refused to behave naturally in response to her advances.

'Why "of course"?'

'We all know we're a bit too ordinary down here in the Port for her taste: vino corriente instead of Rioja.'

'You sound as if you've been drinking vino-agre.'

'Christ! Phil, I'm too boozed for that sort of thing.'

He chuckled.

'Tell me. What d'you think about Dolly?'

'I think the news is a load of cod's. She probably has a thick head this morning, called in the quack, and someone got hold of the wrong end of the stick.'

'You're wrong, wonder-boy. She's dead, all right. No more thick heads for her.'

A plump woman, dressed in a pyjama suit whose seams were under considerable strain, thrust herself into the conversation. 'Wasn't that a just too disgusting scene at her party last night?'

Pam spoke in a drawling, bitchy voice: 'I thought it was the funniest thing I've seen in years.'

'Funny? Boasting about how much money she'd made to poor old Kim when she must have known what happened to his family.'

'Poor old Kim!' she mimicked. 'There's only one thing wrong with him — he's a supercilious bastard.'

'Not one of your many friends, dear?' asked the plump woman sweetly.

A man, holding a glass in each hand and drinking from them alternately, joined them. He stared with bleary eyes at Rockford. 'Hullo, shipmate. How's the voyage going?'

'Come alongside and I'll tell you.'

'Better put your fender out,' said Pam, irritated by this further interruption.

'Suppose you put it out for him, eh?' The man nudged her in the side: some of the drink in one of the glasses slopped over the rim.

'For God's sake,' she snapped. 'You nearly had that down my dress.'

'Can't blame me for trying, love.' He drank. 'Heard the latest about Dolly, I suppose?'

'What about her?' asked the plump woman.

'The police have been called in. They're saying she was murdered.'

Pam laughed sarcastically.

'Straight, it's not just a rumour. I know for a fact that there's been a detective in the house most of the day.'

'But who on earth would murder her?' asked the plump woman, knowing what the answer must be.

'Mark,' answered Pam immediately. 'Not that I thought he had it in him.'

'Steady on with that sort of talk,' said Rockford. 'There's no rhyme or reason for naming him . . .'

'Stop being so judicious. Of course it was him.'

'Aren't you forgetting something? He's in England.'

'Goddamn it, so he is!'

'Then who on earth could it have been?' asked the plump woman, for the second time.

'Kim,' said Pam, and she looked challengingly at Rockford.

By the end of the cocktail-party it was agreed—by those still capable of agreeing anything—that it had been Kim Covert who had murdered Dolly Lund.

CHAPTER 13

Dolores, strikingly handsome in a dark red frock which contrasted sharply with her raven black hair, rested her hands on her hips as she stood by the side of the dining-room table. 'Perhaps you'll just give me an idea of whether you'll be in to lunch today? Of course, it won't matter if you say one thing but change your mind and do another. No matter that I've spent hours slaving in the kitchen . . .'

Alvarez hastily interrupted. 'I tell you, I tried my damndest to get back yesterday, but just couldn't. I had to wait hours for the doctor, then there was the maid to question, the house to search . . .'

'And you ate hardly any supper.'

He tried to follow the logic of her conversation and failed. 'What's that got to do with anything?'

'If you had not eaten any lunch at all, when you got back here you'd have eaten an enormous supper.'

He was reminded of an old Mallorquin saying: 'Beware of the landlord with a sharp wife, the lawyer with a sharp wit, and the woman with a sharp eye.'

'I can't blame you, of course. After all, what is my poor cooking compared to a meal in a grand house?'

He spoke penitently. 'Look, I did eat something. But only because the maid was in such a state and didn't want to be left on her own. She gave me some meat which tasted as if it had died of old age and all the time I was chewing it I thought of your wonderful arroz brut which I was missing.'

'I offered you what was left last night and you only ate enough to keep a flea alive.'

'I know, but the meat had given me terrible indigestion: my guts were twisted up in knots.'

She graciously accepted his explanation, but made him promise that this day he'd be back for lunch—for which she had already started to slave—no matter what state the maid was in. He asked her what she was cooking and then swore that nothing, not even grilled gambas, would prevent his returning for so Lucullan a feast.

He left the house, unlocked the door of his battered Seat 600, and sat behind the wheel. There were usually ways and means of getting around the woman with a sharp eye, but the lawyer with a sharp wit . . .

Vives had bought two flats and turned one into a set of offices. He was a man of medium height, with a face pock-marked by a bad attack of acne when young: his character was warm and his manner friendly. He shook hands, demanded to know why Alvarez hadn't been along months before for a chat, then settled behind his desk, stacked with files and papers, and made it clear that although he was delighted by the meeting, he was a very busy man.

'You drew up a will for Señora Lund . . . Is it good?'

He smiled. 'Everything I do is good.'

'I mean, is it her last will?'

'I imagine so. But if there's any doubt, it's easy enough to check with Madrid to find out.'

'Will you do that for me?'

'Sure.' He made a note on a pad, then looked up. 'What's in the wind?'

'You'll have heard she's dead. It's possible she was murdered. I'm looking for the motive.'

He leaned back in the chair and joined his fingertips together.

'Did she often ask you to do her legal work?'

'This was the first time.'

'What happened?'

'She made an appointment and when I saw her she said she wanted her will drawn up. I checked if she'd made any other will in Spain and as she had I explained that a new one would automatically render null and void that previous one.'

'Did you advise her on the contents of the will?'

'Did I have anything to do with the terms? No way. She knew exactly what she wanted and told me.'

'Did you know she had a daughter?'

'One minute. I think I'd better refresh my memory.' He used the internal telephone to ask one of the secretaries to bring him Señora Lund's file and when that was in front of him he quickly read through the papers inside. 'According to my notes, she told me she hadn't any close living relatives after I'd explained that under Spanish law a Spaniard—but not always a foreigner—had to leave a proportion of the estate—under normal conditions—to certain named relatives.'

'You are quite sure she said she'd no daughter?'

'I've a note to that effect here.'

Alvarez scratched his forehead, at the point where his hair was receding rather quickly. 'Did you know that Mark Erington was her gigolo?'

'She naturally never said so, but I guessed as much.'

'He stands to collect quite a fortune, doesn't he?'

'More money than either you or I will ever see.'

'Did she talk to you about him?'

'I don't remember her doing so and certainly I've no notes referring to him apart from the fact that he was to get virtually everything.'

'What about George Trent?'

'The man who's left the cigarette case?' He shrugged his shoulders. 'I gather he lives locally, but that's all I know about him.'

'She didn't say why she was leaving him a pewter cigarette case?'

'Not a word.'

Alvarez thought for a moment. 'Do you get the feeling there's something odd about the will?'

'I don't know that it's any odder than others I've drawn up.'

'You don't get a suggestion . . .' He stopped, since it was clear that Vives failed to see any special, but as yet unidentified, significance in the terms. 'I wonder why she cut her daughter right out?'

'You're sure there really is a daughter?'

'There's a framed photo of her on the señora's dressing-table.'

Vives began to drum on the desk with his fingers. 'People who've had bitter rows don't usually keep each other's photos on view, do they? But if they were on good, or even reasonable terms, why did the señora deny she had a daughter?'

'You can't suggest the answers?'

He shook his head.

'I was hoping,' said Alvarez despondently.

Matas was sitting on a chair out on the road, wondering whether it had been wise to allow Rosa to go to the Institute to work for her bachillerato?—there were all those male students and since when had any male student had a thought higher than his loins? . . .

'Hullo, old man,' said Alvarez.

He looked up, shielding his eyes with gnarled right hand. 'So it's you . . . Nothing wrong, is there?' he asked with sudden and sharp concern, terrified that Rosa was in trouble—of one sort or another.

'I don't know yet.' Alvarez leaned against the wall of the house. 'Tell me something. How d'you spell puta?'

Matas reached for his pipe, which was under the chair with a battered goatskin tobacco pouch, and began to pack the bowl with tobacco.

'Come on, old 'un.'

'I don't spell nothing. Can't read, nor yet write.'

'Rosa can.'

'Aye, that she can,' he said with pride.

'So she'd tell you?'

'D'you think I'd bloody well ask her to spell a word like that?' he demanded indignantly.

'No, I don't. So I reckon that's why you got it wrong.'

Matas concentrated on lighting the pipe.

'The word has only one T.'

'What's it to me whether it has one or a dozen?'

'Because you spelled it with two on the lawn of Señora Lund.'

'I didn't do no such thing.'

'Must've taken quite a bit of weed killer. Bought a lot recently?'

He sucked at his pipe.

'I'll have to ask around and find out.'

'The old bitch,' said Matas violently. 'Slung me, just on account of taking a few of me own tomatoes.'

'When did you put the weedkiller down?'

'I ain't sayin' I did any such thing.'

'Some time ago? There's been no rain to wash it in, only the dew and there's precious little of that at this time of the year. You weren't able to use the watering system because you could only be around after dark and if they'd heard the pressure pump working for any length of time they'd have wanted to know why. You hoped the grass would be dead by Saturday night when it was the big party, didn't you?'

A lorry rumbled past, its badly adjusted diesel engine briefly drowning out all speech and leaving behind it the acrid smell of the exhaust.

'D'you work at Ca Na Nadana for long?'

'Nigh on two year.'

'Did you know she drank a lot?'

'I'd've had to be blind and deaf not to know that.'

'And she drank even more than usual when she had a party?'

He said nothing.

'Did they ever give you a key to the house?'

' 'Course not.'

'Wouldn't have been much trouble to get a key cut, would it? Or even have taken one and left them to think it was lost so as they'd pay to have another cut if they didn't change the lock.'

'I ain't never had no bleeding key.'
'Don't forget next time. Puta has only one T.'

Alvarez slowly climbed the stairs to his office, conscious of
the fact that if he were in reasonable physical condition
he would not be nearly so out of breath. Too much drink,
too much food, too many cigarettes, too little exercise. All
it needed was enough will power to cut out alcohol and
cigarettes, to refuse second helpings, and to walk to the
guardia post each day instead of using the car.

He entered his room, darkened because the shutters
were closed, and slumped down in the chair behind the
desk. There were times when sadness overwhelmed a man
and gnawed like a rat at his mind. Suppose he were to die
suddenly, now, here, in the chair? Who would there be to
mourn him? Dolores and Jaime, and the two children,
Juan and Isabel, certainly. But their grief would be brief
because the relationship was, in fact, more distant than
cousin and despite all their wonderful kindnesses to him,
kindness was never quite the same thing as love born of
close consanguinity. Apart from them—no one. So he was
an island—which could disappear without leaving a
ripple in the sea of indifference . . . He leaned down and
pulled open the bottom right-hand drawer of the desk to
bring out a bottle of brandy and a glass. Undoubtedly
there were times when just a little alcohol was a man's
best friend . . . His only friend . . .

He rang Palma, spoke to Superior Chief Salas's
superior secretary, and after a long wait was put through
to the great man. He explained very carefully that a
wealthy foreigner had died and the circumstances of her
death were such that although on the face of things it had
been accidental, it was possible she had, in fact, been
murdered.

Salas spoke with weary annoyance. 'Why?' he asked,
repeating the word after a slight pause, 'why is it that of

all my officers it is you, Inspector Alvarez, who never knows anything for certain?'

'Señor, in this case . . .'

'If someone is sought, you know only that he may be here or he may be there: if someone is certainly missing, you know only that he may be alive or he may be dead: if someone is dead, you know only that he may have died from natural causes, from accidental causes, or from being murdered.'

'Señor, until the post mortem has confirmed the doctor's findings it is impossible for anyone to be certain.'

'I have not the slightest doubt that even then you will successfully discover an ocean of ambiguity.'

After the call was over, Alvarez finished the brandy. He sighed as he put the now empty glass on the desk. The phone buzzed. He ignored it. It buzzed again and with an expression of annoyance he lifted the receiver. 'What is it?'

'It's Victoriana here, señor. You know, Ca Na Nadana. There's been a telephone call from the airport and I just didn't know what to say and . . .'

'A call from who, señorita?'

'From Señor Erington. He wanted to speak to the señora. I was so bewildered and upset that . . . I couldn't think what . . .'

'Did you say she was dead?'

'I didn't. I kept wondering what to say and in the end he rang off. I think he thought I'd been drinking.'

'As far as you know, is he driving straight to the house from the airport?'

'I think so, señor.'

'I'll be over to be there when he arrives.'

Alvarez crossed the lawn of Ca Na Nadana to the west-facing covered patio. From behind him came the rattle of stones being unloaded into a wheelbarrow. As Victoriana

had said, repeatedly, old Angel Matas might sometimes
be difficult, but at least he was a Lluesian: in sharp and
unwelcome contrast, Ripoli—unmistakably a man of
Mestara—was young, cocky, a know-all, and, since he
came from that village, untrustworthy. Unfortunately,
while Alvarez would willingly have disbelieved what he'd
just been told, Ripoli's sly grin had been full of scornful
confidence. He had, he'd said, spent the weekend,
together with his family, with his wife's parents ('Very full
of money!'). So he knew absolutely nothing about what
had happened in Ca Na Nadana. And if Alvarez didn't
believe him—people from Llueso were notoriously
suspicious—all he had to do was to speak to his wife's
parents ('She was their only child. With all that wealth!')
and they'd confirm every word he said . . .

Alvarez entered the house and as he did so Victoriana
called out: 'There's a car just driven in.' He went through
to the hall, opened the front door.

A red Seat 124 Sport, hood down, had just parked in
front of the double garage and Erington, dressed in open-
neck safari shirt, linen trousers, and sandals, was opening
the boot of the car. He saw Alvarez and straightened up.
'Who are you? Where's Victoriana?'

Alvarez crossed to the car and briefly introduced
himself.

'A . . . a detective.' Erington looked past him at the
house. 'What the hell's going on? Victoriana sounded as if
she'd lost her wits. Where's Dolly . . . Señora Lund?'

'Señor, I fear I have some bad news for you.'

'Bad news?'

'Señora Lund died last night.' He watched Erington's
face.

Erington looked shocked, then disbelieving. 'Impossible.'

'I assure you, señor, that regrettably it is true.'

'Dolly . . . Dolly's dead?'

He nodded. Perhaps Erington had mistaken his vocation and should have gone in for acting?

'But . . . but what did she die from?'

'Shall we go inside and then I will tell you.'

Erington, seemingly bewildered, picked up his suitcase out of the boot and followed Alvarez into the house. 'I'll just take my case up to my room.'

Alvarez made no objection and Erington went upstairs. When he returned he said abruptly, as he entered the sitting-room: 'Her room's locked.'

'Indeed, señor.'

'Why?'

'I have locked it.'

'What makes you think you've any right to do that?'

'Perhaps you will understand when I tell you that it is possible the señora was murdered.'

'What? . . . That's ridiculous. She can't have been.'

'No one can know for certain until medical tests have been completed, but in the meantime I have unfortunately to assume that she was.'

'Why? Simply because she swallowed a whole load of sleeping pills . . .' He stopped abruptly.

'Señor, I have mentioned nothing about why she died so how did you know that she had taken sleeping pills?'

He spoke hoarsely. 'I didn't. I just assumed it.'

'Then why should you have made such an assumption?'

'Because she would keep taking them though I went on and on about the danger of doing that after she'd been drinking. Look, you've got to understand that when I arrived here just now I didn't have the slightest idea she'd died, far less that anyone suspected she'd been murdered. But I did know that when she gives a party she always drinks too much and when she goes to bed she falls asleep immediately, but invariably wakes up during the night and then can't get back to sleep. So she takes sleeping pills even though the doctor and I have both warned her how terribly dangerous that can be . . . I didn't *know* anything, but after what you'd said I could guess. D'you see that?'

'Of course.'

'God, I need a drink! Hell of a shock . . . What about you?'

'I think not, thank you.'

Erington went over to the mobile cocktail cabinet and poured himself out a whisky and soda. 'I want some ice and Victoriana hasn't put any out yet . . .' He looked at Alvarez, then left the room. When he returned, his glass was already half empty. 'You said that maybe Dolly was murdered. But who on earth could possibly want to kill her?'

'Señor, if necessary it will become my job to find out.'

He drank. The whisky began to restore some of his confidence and he spoke much more easily. 'I'm afraid it's true she wasn't all that popular with some people. She . . . Well, to tell the truth, she couldn't be bothered to make the effort to be pleasant to people she didn't particularly like. But for God's sake, you don't kill someone just because you dislike her, do you? So what possible motive could there be?'

'I suppose that the señora was a very rich person?'

'I imagine so.'

'You do not know for sure?'

'Dolly could be very secretive at times.'

'You are saying that she did not speak to you about money?'

'Never. That is, except . . .' He squared his shoulders. 'You'll probably have already learned that I live here but Dolly pays . . . paid . . . all the bills?'

Alvarez said nothing.

'So there were just a few occasions when we did discuss money. But it was never generally: always specifically. I've no idea of how rich she was.'

'Can you say who will inherit the señora's fortune?'

'It'll almost certainly be Samantha, her daughter. There's been quite a row between them, but Dolly's not the kind of person to forget the ties of blood.'

'There has been a row?'

'Samantha is very independent: Dolly was inclined to be possessive. I suppose it's a fairly common cause for friction.'

'Have you met the señora's daughter?'

There was a brief pause. 'Yes. She married a man whom Dolly really disliked and that caused a breach. Unfortunately, Dolly turned out to be right and the man was a rotter who'd thought that by marrying Samantha he'd be marrying Dolly's money. When he discovered that wasn't so, he left her. Dolly was naturally upset and after a time she asked me to find out how Samantha was—she was too proud to ask me to try to heal the breach between them, but that's what she wanted.'

'Señor, I am a little puzzled. I was told by Victoriana that the daughter was married to a very successful businessman?'

'Yes, I imagine you were.' He hesitated, then said: 'I suppose with Dolly dead the truth's going to have to come out. But I'd hate to be the one responsible for the local bitches learning about it after all her kindness . . . Will you promise to keep as much as possible of what I tell you confidential?'

'Of course.'

'Dolly was wealthy—it doesn't matter exactly how wealthy: as I've said, I can't answer that. Being wealthy one would have thought she'd have been completely self-assured, but in fact she suffered from an inferiority complex because of her social background—it was very different from the social background of many of the people who live here. The English didn't invent snobbery, but they elevated it to a fine art and that sort of attitude still lingers on here. Dolly was frightened that she'd suffer a social black eye if people learned that her daughter was married to a fortune-seeker who'd left her, so she invented a socially desirable and very successful husband.'

Alvarez rubbed his chin. It was all very odd! 'When you saw the señora's daughter, was she ready to be friendly with her mother once more?'

'She was still resentful, of course, but underneath that resentment there was a longing to bury the hatchet. If this hadn't happened now . . .' He shrugged his shoulders. 'But it's happened. Nobody can turn the clock back.'

'Thank you for your help, señor.'

'That's all right . . . Look, I wonder if you can help me.' His manner became slightly embarrassed.

'If I can.'

'It's a question of where I stand. I mean, with Dolly dead can I go on living here until I've made a few arrangements or ought I to leave immediately?'

'I think that is a question which you must put to the señora's solicitor, Señor Vives.'

'You mean Señor Borobia.'

'Señor Vives, who practises in the village.'

'But . . .' He stared at Alvarez, frowning.

Alvarez said goodbye and walked towards the door. He stopped, turned. 'Señor, how is your mother?'

'My mother . . . ?' For a moment the question seemed to puzzle him, then he said hurriedly: 'It wasn't nearly as serious as the telegram suggested, thank God. If I'd rung through to find out exactly how things were before I did anything else, I'd probably have stayed on for the party. I suppose . . . I suppose if I'd been here Saturday night that would have saved Dolly from being murdered. It doesn't make an easy thought to live with.'

CHAPTER 14

Alvarez returned to Ca Na Nadana and parked next to the open Seat, which had been left outside the garage. He rang the front-door bell and as he waited he turned round and stared at the field beyond the drive in which a crop of barley, grown under fig and almond trees, had very recently been harvested. Fifty years ago, he thought, all suitable land had been used to grow food and people had been poor and hungry: today, much of the best land had either been buried under concrete or turned into gardens and yet few people were poor and none needed to be hungry. How could any man understand life when it presented such a paradox?

The door was opened by Ana. His first emotion on seeing her was one of quiet compassion: Ana was so very plain when compared to Victoriana. But there was a ring on her engagement finger. Victoriana, beautiful and vivacious, longed for what she probably would never have: Ana, plain, dull, was happily content with the little she had. Another paradox?

She told him the señor was outside and showed him through to the pool patio. Erington lay sunbathing by the side of the pool and when he heard them he came to his feet. 'Thanks a lot for coming here so promptly. Thing was, I reckoned you must be told as soon as possible: matter of fact, that old shark, Vives, thought the same . . . You'll have a drink this time, won't you?' He walked round to the west-facing house patio and pressed the bell push by the side of the telephone extension socket. 'We might as well sit down here, in the shade. When the sun gets this hot, I have to admit that even I can get too much of it.'

They sat at the glass-topped bamboo table. Erington produced a thin gold cigarette case which contained cigarettes with different coloured paper. 'They're all the same tobacco—just a bit of nonsense, really, but it's quite amusing.'

Alvarez took a green cigarette. Ana came out, followed by Lulu, and Erington asked her to wheel out the drinks. As she returned inside, Lulu sniffed Alvarez's trousers and after a thoughtful pause wagged her tail because she realized she knew him. He bent down and patted her: the moment he stopped, she waddled under the table to Erington, who lifted her on to his lap.

'I saw Vives, as I mentioned over the phone,' said Erington. 'He told me . . . I still can't believe it. But you must know something about the terms of the will or you wouldn't have been so hot on my going to see him . . . She's left everything to me. It's . . . I just can't get used to the fact.'

'You had no idea, señor?'

'Of course I didn't,' he answered sharply. 'How could I have?'

'There is a copy of the señora's will in this house.'

'There is? . . . How d'you find that out?'

'It is in the desk in the study.'

'In Dolly's desk. Good God!'

'Do you not have spare keys to her desk?'

'I do not. That study was Dolly's sanctum sanctorum and no one else was allowed near it except to dust . . . D'you mind telling me how you managed to open the desk?'

'With the keys which were kept in the toes of a shoe in a cupboard in the señora's bedroom.'

Ana wheeled out the cocktail cabinet and told Erington that the ice beaker was full, she'd emptied a tin of olives into a dish which was on the top shelf, and there was a sliced lemon on a plate.

Erington poured out a brandy and soda for Alvarez and a Cinzano and soda for himself. He raised his glass in salute, drank. 'I don't want to make too much of it, but I do wonder if you had the right to search for those keys and, having found them, to open the desk and read the papers inside?'

'Señor, the police in Spain have many rights.'

'I don't think that really answers my question.' He waited, then said: 'Did you look through all the papers in the desk?'

'I have not as yet, but I will be doing so.'

'But I'm sure those are all her personal papers.'

'If the señora was killed I am afraid nothing of hers can be held to be private until the murderer is identified.'

'It's a rotten business,' he said with sudden passion. 'How she'd hate knowing that all her secrets are in danger of becoming public knowledge. It makes the whole business seem even more ghastly and sordid than it already is.'

'Indeed,' agreed Alvarez somberly. 'Now, señor, you have something to tell me?'

'How d'you mean?'

'You suggested over the telephone that I came here to speak to you.'

'Yes, because of the will. I was sure you'd want to know what the terms are . . . But since then I've realized you must already know them . . . I'm afraid I've not been thinking very straight.'

'When a man has been shocked, it is often very difficult for him to think correctly.'

Erington was afraid that the words had been spoken ironically, but Alvarez's expression remained bland, even a little vacant.

Alvarez finished his drink. 'Señor, may I now have permission to examine all the doors of the house?'

Erington answered with some bitterness. 'From what

you said earlier, it doesn't seem to matter whether or not I
give my permission.'

'Yet it is far more satisfactory to us both if you do.'

'Typically Spanish—the sting is in the tail . . . Look
wherever you want.'

'You are very kind.'

'But in return, just tell me one thing. What in the devil
are you looking for?'

'The signs of a forced entry. If there are such signs, we
know how and where an intruder broke in: if there are
none, we have to ask ourselves, why not?'

He had brought with him a lock probe—a tiny tube
with a minute bulb and a mirror, attached to a battery—which enabled an observer to look into the heart of
a lock to check whether there were any traces in the oil or
grease in those parts of the lock which had not been made
shiny by the use of the key. With the probe in his right
hand, and the battery in his left, he inspected the lock of
the top drawer of the kneehole desk in the study. There
were numerous scratches to show that the lock had been
forced, either very clumsily once or fairly expertly on
many occasions. It was the same with the lock of the top
left-hand narrow drawer, to the side of the kneehole.

He left the study and walked round the outside of the
house, visually inspecting the locks of all the doors. None
of them showed the slightest sign of ever having been
forced. He went upstairs and checked the two doors
which gave access to the small upstairs patios, one at
either end of the house: they had not been touched
either. So, assuming that Victoriana had fastened all the
shutters and locked all the doors on Saturday night before
she went to bed, as she claimed to have done, the only
way now left of forcibly breaking into the house was via
the top, open floor.

He unlocked the door of the master bedroom, crossed
to the nearest window, opened the shutters—with the air-

conditioning off, the windows had been left open — and leaned out, but not very far since he was a lifelong sufferer from altophobia, and judged distances. It would require a ladder of at least six and a half metres to reach the top floor . . . While it couldn't positively be ruled out that such a ladder had been brought and used, it did not seem likely.

He thankfully withdrew into the room and as he did so his attention was caught by a scratch on the glass of the left-hand window which had been swung back. When he looked more closely, he realized there were two scratches, roughly parallel, a couple of centimetres apart, half a metre long. Had there, then, been an attempt to break in through this window? Yet the shutters had been closed and fastened and a careful examination now confirmed that no attempt had ever been made to force them . . . Fool, he suddenly thought, meaning himself. If he had had more than half his wits about him, he'd have realized from the beginning that the scratches were on the inside of the glass, not the outside!

He looked round the bedroom once more, sighed because he had learned nothing fresh, closed the shutters to return the room to a soft twilight, and then left. After locking the door, he went downstairs to the study.

He sat in front of the desk, unlocked the top, long drawer, and sorted through the scramble of papers. There were bank statements and lists of investments which made him wonder if extra noughts had been slipped in by mistake: there were a few bills which could have meant nothing in the face of such riches: there were respectful letters from banks, stock and commodity brokers, real estate agents: there were half a dozen letters from Samantha.

When he read these half-dozen letters, he had consciously to overcome his reluctance to intrude into the privacy of the two women: and to begin with he briefly

examined them with nervous speed, as if he were scared
of being caught indulging in a degraded curiosity. Each
of the letters was without an address. The envelopes of
two of them were badly creased although the sheets of
paper inside were not. He imagined the mother, scornfully crumpling up the envelope and meaning to do the
same with the letter inside, but then being emotionally
caught and held by the contents and keeping both. The
postmarks didn't correspond with the letters inside in
three cases: he could see Samantha, having written the
letter, hesitating for days to send it because her pride still
battled with her despair even though it was doomed to
lose . . .

The first letter, dated some eighteen months before,
was challenging in tone: yes, it was quite true, Paul had
gone to Bristol, but that was simply because friends had
said there was a job for him there: as soon as he was
settled, she was going to join him . . . The second and
third letters, written at intervals of three months, were no
longer challenging but filled with a growing self-pity.
Paul hadn't written or even rung up: every time she tried
to get in touch with him, he seemed to be out: she left
messages which he surely must have received, yet he'd not
answered one of them. She'd been told Paul was seeing
rather a lot of a redhead. There couldn't be anything in
that, but it was rotten of him to spend time with a
redhead and not bother to get in touch with her . . . The
fourth and fifth letters had been written within two weeks
of each other. Paul had left her for the redhead and the
one time she'd managed to have a word with him, begging him to return home, he'd brutally told her to get
lost. She'd become ill with worry and despair. She'd
had to give up her work because she couldn't cope. The
national health doctor couldn't, or wouldn't, do anything
more than put her on tranquillizers, which were utterly
useless. She owed money on the rent of the flat and the

landlord was trying to throw her out, in spite of the legal
protection all tenants were supposed to have. She couldn't
pay the grocery bills. She'd heard of a psychiatrist who did
wonders for people who'd reached the state she was in,
but he only worked privately and was expensive. She and
Dolly had had their rows, especially over Paul and how
she wished she'd listened to Dolly's advice! Dolly had been
quite right—he was just a working-class rotter. Please,
please could Dolly let her have a little money to help her
out of her troubles? If only she could afford to see the
psychiatrist . . . Attached to the sixth letter was a
torn sheet of paper on which was writing that Alvarez
recognized as the señora's. He read and knew a sharp,
bitter anger. That any woman could dream of writing
thus to her own daughter. 'Hardly any money' . . . When
her bank statements and lists of investments were so heavy
that the paper they were printed on was strained. 'You've
made your bed and now must lie on it' . . . As her mother,
she had helped to make that bed . . . This last letter from
Samantha was tragic. Why had Dolly become so cruel?
She knew she'd married Paul against her mother's wishes,
but that was in the past and couldn't it now be forgotten?
All she'd asked for was just enough money to help her pull
herself together . . . The cheap paper on which the letter
was written was still slightly corrugated in two places,
marking the fall of tears.

He replaced the letters in the drawer. He hated
violence, but for once it seemed to him that murder
might have been justified. If only the motive had been an
overwhelming sense of moral values rather than sordid
gain . . .

The Institute of Forensic Anatomy telephoned Alvarez at
seven-forty-five that evening.

'Professor Fortunato,' said a plummy-voiced woman,
'has completed his post mortem. He has asked me to give

you his findings verbally, although naturally I shall be sending you a typed copy of the report later on. Do you wish to take notes?'

He was reminded of the elderly, buck-toothed woman who had once—and somewhat unavailingly—tried to teach him arithmetic. 'I'm ready, señorita.'

'The deceased died from asphyxia, occasioned by something soft, made of linen, being pressed over her mouth and nostrils: a pillow, perhaps. Particles containing linen were found in the air passages . . .'

When she had finished, he asked: 'Can you say how much she had drunk?'

'Her blood/alcohol level was just under point three.'

'Then she was as tight as a tick?'

He should have realized that this was not the sort of expression of which she would approve. 'The deceased was in a state of severe intoxication.'

'And what about the sleeping pills: how many had she taken?'

'Only the preliminary tests have been carried out. They suggest that the deceased had taken no form of sleeping drugs within the past twenty-four hours. It will be some considerable time before the final tests can be completed.'

'These preliminary tests . . . How likely are they to turn out wrong?'

'Most unlikely,' she snapped, as if she personally had carried them out and therefore his question was insulting.

He thanked her, received a frosty goodbye, and rang off. Where had the nineteen pills got to? If the señora had opened the bottle and in doing so had spilled them out, surely she would never have bothered to search for them and pick them up in the drunken state in which she'd been? Yet there'd not been one on the floor. If she hadn't swallowed any, why had she ever opened the bottle? Were they wrong in assuming the bottle to have been a new one? Yet the presence of the container and the instructions pamphlet taken together with Victoriana's evidence suggested that it must have been . . . If the señora had been stifled with a pillow, did it matter a solitary damn whether it was a new or an old bottle and whether none or all nineteen pills were unaccounted for?

He looked at the telephone, knew what he had to do and funked doing it for several minutes, then dialled Palma and spoke to Salas's secretary. She, at her most superior, said she would see if the superior chief were free. Alvarez waited, determined to forget the pills. Inevitably, he racked his brains to work out a logical way in which nineteen of them could vanish.

'Yes?' said Salas, already impatient.

'Señor, I think I can now make a preliminary report . . .'

'Can you or can't you? If you can, do so: if you can't, get off the line.'

'The thing is that to date I've had only a preliminary report from the Institute of Forensic Anatomy . . .'

'Was the señora murdered?'

'That is now certain and . . .'

'With sleeping pills?'

'No, señor. In fact, she was suffocated, perhaps with a pillow. You see . . .'

'Did you not previously report that she'd taken too many sleeping pills after drinking a large quantity of alcohol?'

'It now seems she did not take any sleeping pills. I was mistaken.'

'A distressingly common occurrence. Who murdered her?'

'She had a young man living with her and she's left all her money to him. Although he claims to have been in England on the night of her death, I feel it is very likely that he was the murderer.'

'Have you arrested him?'

'Not yet, señor. I still have to discuss his alibi with him . . .'

'Good God! Are you now confessing you haven't even had the initiative to do that as yet?'

If he hadn't phoned, Alvarez thought, he'd have been in trouble: because he had phoned, he was in trouble. He leaned over and reached down to the right-hand bottom drawer of the desk.

CHAPTER 15

Alvarez drove off the road on to the dirt track and stopped in front of the caseta on the left, situated roughly a hundred metres before the T-junction, the right-hand fork of which led on to Ca Na Nadana. He turned into the rough gateway.

The scene was one to bring him warm pleasure. The stone caseta was old, small, and primitively simple: a kitchen, a living-room, and a bedroom. There was a patio which consisted of a cobbled floor, rough concrete pillars, and a criss-cross of rusty wire over which grew two vines which gave cool, dancing shade and the promise of a bountiful harvest of grapes. Beyond the patio was a well, surrounded by a rampart which a donkey or mule would endlessly circle as it turned a large wheel equipped with clay pots which lifted up the water and discharged it to flow into an estanque. The land was intensely cultivated: tomatoes, aubergines, sweet peppers, lettuces, peanuts, chick peas, beans and melons were growing in lush profusion. Contented grunts from a pig-sty identified a litter of pigs being fattened: hobbled sheep and chickens gleaned the stubble to the side of the vegetables: a tethered goat grazed on brambles. A man had begun to plough the stubble with a mule and a Roman plough: a woman was drawing irrigation channels with a mattock . . . Here was the real Mallorca.

The woman reached the end of the row, stood upright, and stared at him: the man brought the mule to a halt and did the same. He walked past the estanque, by the side of which were rows of cut and washed lettuces ready for the market, and came up to the woman. 'How are things, then?'

She shaded her eyes with a calloused hand and studied him. 'It's Enrique. We've not seen you for many a moon.' It was a flat statement of fact, expressing no emotion.

'It must have been at Margarita's wedding.'

She nodded.

Cardell, who'd tied the mule up to a fig tree, walked across with slow, deliberate strides. 'It's Enrique,' he said, unknowingly echoing his wife's words. They shook hands.

They talked about the weather, the state of the crops, and in particular the low prices those crops were fetching. There was no bitterness in their voices: life had always been hard and unrewarding and the prosperity of the tourist boom had touched them only lightly. They asked him to take a glass of wine with them—since they would have been having a break anyway—and they all sat under the vines and drank rough wine which the couple had made the previous harvest.

'You know the English señora up the road died last Saturday night?' said Alvarez.

They nodded. They had heard, but the information was of small interest: rich foreigners lived in a totally different world.

'It's possible she was murdered so I've got to try and find out who did it . . . Early Sunday morning, it was, about four. I was wondering if either of you was awake then?'

They looked at each other and eventually Cardell said:

'She had toothache.' The woman nodded: she had had bad toothache, but it was not something one normally bothered to talk about because the whole of life was pain.

'There's nothing worse than toothache,' said Alvarez commiseratingly. 'Hope you've had it fixed up?'

She made no answer.

'Did it keep you awake?'

'Aye.'

'D'you hear anyone coming along the lane during the night and specially around four?'

She thought for a long while and Cardell picked up the earthenware pitcher and refilled their glasses with wine.

'Earlier on there were many cars,' she finally said.

They would have been the guests leaving Ca Na Nadana after the party was finished. 'What about after them?'

'Juan the butcher went by.'

He did not ask how she could be so certain of the driver's identity: they would know the noises which certain cars made as they bumped along the uneven surface. 'Was that late?'

'Before twelve.' At night time they could hear the striking of the clock in the church in the square in Llueso, unless the wind was from the north.

'What about after twelve?' he asked with the endless patience of a peasant.

'There was a Mobylette.'

'When?'

'Just after two.'

'Who owns a Mobylette up this road?' He knew that by Mobylette they meant any of the motorized bicycles.

Between them, they mentioned three men and one woman.

'Do they live up the track?'

Cardell said that the four had fields in which they

worked during the days, but they all lived in houses in the village.

'Did you hear the Mobylette return?'

'It came by just after the half-hour.'

'What about after that?'

'Nothing.'

'And you were awake around four?'

She nodded.

Alvarez finished his wine, talked once more about the crops, then thanked them and said he'd be moving on. They were glad: they never spent long resting.

He drove slowly up to the T-junction, his thoughts confused. Erington would have been in a car, assuming he had made a brief, secret flight to Palma on the Saturday night. Yet Carolina Cardell had not heard any vehicle after the Mobylette at half past two. Of course, she might have slept much more than she imagined she had and the car might have passed in both directions as she did so. Again, the doctor had stressed how inaccurate the estimated time of death could be—but he had made his estimate only five hours after death and in such circumstances to be one and a half hours out seemed rather a lot . . .

He drove past Ca Na Nadana to Ca'n Bispo. Rockford opened the door and he introduced himself and was immediately asked inside. Cynthia was in the sitting-room, seated in one of the armchairs, and she nodded at him with the imperious grace with which any well connected English lady greeted the unimportant and the poor.

'Señora,' he said, in answer to her nod, 'I must sincerely apologize for bothering you at such a time of the evening.'

She ignored him. 'No bother at all,' said Rockford heartily. 'Sit down over there . . . What'll you have to drink?'

'I think nothing, thank you,' he replied, as he settled on

the settee. 'I have just taken some homemade wine and I do not think much else will settle happily with it.'

Rockford laughed. 'I've had some of that in the past and I reckon you're just about right! There was that bottle of plonk I bought in Aden — before it became independent, of course . . .'

'Not again, surely?' said Cynthia.

Rockford said cheerfully: 'I'm afraid my wife's heard all my stories more than once. For her, it's a case of twice told, pales.'

'Señor?' said Alvarez politely.

'Well, you see, it should be twice told tales, but I . . . I'm sorry, but I don't think it's really going to be possible to explain. Plays on words are very difficult to explain or translate, aren't they?'

'Indeed.'

'I often think that that's one of the reasons why countries end up fighting each other. A sense of humour is necessary for getting along even in everyday life, so when you get two nations trying to co-exist it's infinitely more important. But the trouble is, what strikes an Englishman as rather punny merely seems very fou-lish to a Frenchman.'

'My God!' exclaimed Cynthia shrilly. 'Haven't I suffered enough?' She slapped her book shut, stood, and left the sitting-room by turning right into the corridor which led to the two bedrooms.

'I'm afraid she's rather overwrought,' said Rockford, now contrite. 'It's not that we were ever close friends of Dolly, but to have something like that happen next door . . . I suppose it is true that she was murdered?'

'I am afraid that that was confirmed today, señor.'

'It gets a woman all on edge, you know, even when you tell 'em that lightning never strikes twice. I've had to put new locks on all the doors and shut the windows at night even though it makes the rooms stuffier than a gunroom in the tropics. So you'll have to excuse her . . .'

'There is absolutely nothing to excuse.'

'Kind of you . . . Don't mind if I have a quick tot, do you? Matter of fact, I was just going to pour myself a brandy when you arrived. One thing about Spain, the inflation curve may have headed up into the heavens, but with the pound strong for once one can still afford to drink. Can't back home, you know.' He crossed to the wooden chest and opened this. 'If I lived in England, I might be able to stretch to a pint of bitter at the weekend, but that would be my limit.' He carried his glass through to the kitchen where he added soda and ice. He spoke through the open hatchway. 'You said you wanted to ask me a few questions because I might be able to help you. Fire away.'

Alvarez waited until Rockford had returned and was seated in an armchair and then he said: 'Señor, as I told you, we now know that Señora Lund was murdered early on Sunday morning. What I need to discover is if anyone arrived in her house after the party was finished. I have spoken to the old couple who live near the road and because the wife was not well she was awake and heard a Mobylette go by. I want to find out how far up this track it came. Were either you or your wife awake during the night?'

'I know I wasn't. Put my head down and that was that—nothing like champagne to make me sleep soundly.'

'And the señora?'

He chuckled. 'She didn't drink as much as I did, as she made quite a point of telling me, but she was the same. Neither of us flashed an eyelid before nine.'

'Then you cannot help me any further and I will thank you and leave and not bother you any more.'

'You won't change your mind about a quick noggin?'

'Señor, I would enjoy it, but the wine would not.'

'People who say that all wine's safe to drink ought to try that plonk from Aden. Matured in old boots. But we drank it . . . When you're young, you don't worry, do you?'

As he returned to his car, Alvarez sadly thought that when one was young one really didn't worry about anything because the future was such a very long way away. When Rockford had married, had he worried about what his wife would be like in the years to come? Could he have foreseen a thin, icy woman as comfortable as a prickly pear cactus . . . ?

He sat behind the wheel and looked at his watch. It was becoming late, but Salas was an impatient man. So did he now start questioning the owners of the land which lay further up the track to discover whether it had been one of them who had ridden a Mobylette at two in the morning on Sunday? But the men would probably be out at the bars and the women would be cooking and none of them would willingly answer his questions. So perhaps he'd better speak to Trent and try to discover whether there really was something odd about the señora's will.

CHAPTER 16

Carol left the pavement and walked into the garage: she crossed to where Trent was working on the engine of a Citroën. 'I thought it might interest you to be reminded that we once had a date for eight o'clock,' she said, her tone waspish.

He straightened up, wiped the perspiration from his forehead with the back of his hand, and looked at the wall clock which was just visible in the small office. 'I didn't realize it was this late.'

'I quite understand. You weren't worrying about me

but were thinking only of the job.'

'Look, Carol . . .'

She allowed her exasperation full rein. 'Why do you go on and on letting the beastly man exploit you like this?'

He answered wearily. 'Because the only job I'm any good at is a mechanic and because none of the other garages or hire firms want to know me.'

'Then move to somewhere where you can demand what you're worth . . . For God's sake, you're not cut out to be an underpaid mechanic. You've got drive, initiative . . .'

'Will you write out my references?'

'Sometimes I could kick you, very, very hard.'

'Where it really hurts?'

She stared at him and suddenly laughed. He finally smiled in sympathy.

'That's better: you're beginning to look human.'

As she finished speaking, Alvarez entered. He nodded politely at her, then spoke to Trent. 'I have been told that an Englishman of the name of George Trent works here?'

'That's right. Only if you're looking for a car to hire, it's too late. The boss has gone back to his mansion and I'm about to shut up shop and return to my garret. But if you'd like to call in tomorrow morning any time after eight . . .'

'Are you Señor Trent?'

'What if I am?'

'My name is Inspector Alvarez, from the Cuerpo General de Policia.'

Trent tried to appear unworried, but his very unconcern betrayed him.

'Perhaps we might have a talk together?'

'Can't it wait? It's late.'

'I shall not detain you for long.'

'What are you on about?'

'Shall we leave here and find a café and have a coffee together? It will be more pleasant.'

'I want to come,' Carol said abruptly.

Alvarez turned. 'Señorita, nothing would give me greater pleasure.'

Trent said he'd wash and change and he disappeared for a short time. When he returned, he was dressed in loose shirt and jeans. He locked up the garage.

Alvarez led the way to a café on the Llueso/Puerto Llueso road and they sat down at one of the outside tables, set on the pavement. 'The view is not nice, as it is from one of the front cafés,' said Alvarez, 'but the prices are not nearly as high. I console myself with that fact.'

A waiter came up and he asked them if they'd like a drink as well as coffee: they refused. Alvarez ordered three coffees.

'All right,' said Trent roughly, as the waiter went inside. 'What's the trouble? Someone denounced me, I suppose?'

'Why should anyone do that?' replied Alvarez blandly.

Trent cursed himself for a fool.

'Señor, you will have heard that an Englishwoman, Señora Lund, died last Saturday night, or should I say early Sunday morning?'

'Someone mentioned something about it.'

'Have you also heard that she was murdered?'

'My God, no!'

'I just didn't believe it . . .' It was clear Carol had heard the rumour: equally clear that she had not passed it on.

'You knew the señora, did you not?'

Trent stared at the passing traffic. 'No.'

'Are you sure?'

'I've just said, haven't I?'

Carol murmured something in an undertone. The waiter returned with three cups of coffee, three packets of sugar, and a jug of milk. Alvarez offered a pack of cigarettes: Carol accepted a cigarette, Trent refused with a sullen shake of the head. Alvarez struck a match for

Carol and himself, blew it out and dropped it in an ash tray, stirred the contents of a pack of sugar into his coffee. 'Señor, I think that what you have just said is not completely correct. You knew the señora a little?'

'No.'

'Then why should she have mentioned you in her will?'

'She's done what? . . . Not in terms you can repeat, that's for sure.' He suddenly took Carol's cigarette from her and began to smoke it. After a moment, he added: 'All right, I did know the old bitch a bit.' He dropped the cigarette on to the pavement and ground it out under his heel, oblivious of the fact that it had been Carol's.

'In her will she has left you a cigarette case. It is made from pewter.'

'Yeah?'

'Do you know why she has left you this?'

'How in the hell would I?'

'There is not some special sentimental story attached to it?'

'Sentiment was an unknown word where she was concerned.'

'I have understood this. So now I am curious to find out what is so special about the cigarette case.'

'I don't know. And as far as I am concerned you can take it and shove it where the monkey shoves its nuts.'

'George, please don't get so uptight,' pleaded Carol, trying to stop him antagonizing a detective.

'Señor, I have arranged to be given the cigarette case which was clearly described in the will. If I show it to you now, will you say if you have ever seen it before?' Alvarez brought the case from his trouser pocket and laid it on the table.

Trent stared at it. 'Never clapped eyes on it before. But I can tell you one thing, wherever that came from, she didn't have it for long. She only went in for gold or platinum.'

Alvarez, believing Trent, tried to make sense of the facts. 'Señor, will you tell me when you first met Señora Lund?'

'Soon after I arrived in the Port.' His voice had sharpened.

'How was it that you met her?'

'That's my affair.'

'George . . .' began Carol.

'Look, I've never seen that cigarette case before so what she was doing leaving it to me in her will I don't know and I don't bloody care. There's the end of it.'

'I think not quite, señor. There is something it is necessary for me to understand. Please tell me, where and how did you meet her?'

'Didn't you get the message? It's my business and it's staying that way.'

Alvarez continued to speak quietly and politely, but now there was authority in his voice. 'When I spoke to you in the garage, you seemed worried: when we first came here, you assumed that someone had denounced you. Why?'

'Because in this country half the population spends its time denouncing the other half.'

'But why should you feel you are in a position to be denounced? Is it, perhaps, that you do not have a work permit, even though you work in a garage?'

Trent's expression became sullen.

'Señor, I think that perhaps it would be best if you tell me the truth.'

'Christ! You people don't believe in giving anyone a sporting chance, do you? Like the bulls.' He hesitated, then spoke to Carol. 'Suppose you take a bit of a walk . . .'

'Suppose I don't,' she replied tightly.

'Don't you understand?'

'I understand that if we're to go on respecting each other, I've got to know. Whatever it is.'

He swallowed heavily, looked back at the traffic. Then slowly, in a dull voice, he told them. He'd arrived in the Port, with so little money that eating was a luxury, to be almost dazed by the beauty of the place, so dramatically different from the slums he'd left only a fortnight before, when the firm he'd worked for ever since leaving school had made him redundant. For a man who'd reckoned he knew what the world was all about, he'd been strangely naive. He'd thought that because he was a skilled mechanic, he'd get work easily. He learned quickly. There were work permits and foreigners who didn't have one either didn't work or else agreed to work at well below the minimum wage. He could, of course, have returned to the UK and lived on the dole, but he was a fighter: and in any case he had learned the disturbing truth, unknown to all his friends back home, that there were places where life did not consist of squalor, booze-ups, and constant confrontations between them and us.

Dolly had telephoned the car hire firm for which he'd worked that first summer—it wasn't the one where he now was—and he'd been told to drive a Seat 132 up to her place: she had only had one car then and it had broken down. The maid had told him to give her the keys and she'd hand them on to the señora, but he'd replied that he had to see the señora because she had to sign the insurance form. He'd been shown into the sitting-room. And there he'd waited, getting angrier and angrier as the minutes passed because the rich were so contemptuous of other people's feelings. Finally, Dolly had come into the room. Dressed as if off to a fashion show, she'd looked at him with surprise before smiling and asking what he'd like to drink while she signed whatever it was he wanted her to sign.

'I always thought I was wide awake, but when it came to her I was still wet behind the ears.' He spoke as if still astonished by what had happened. 'D'you know what I thought about her right then? No fooling. Here's one rich old bag who's different: actually doesn't reckon the money puts her up above the angels.' He picked up the cup and finished the coffee.

'You saw her again?' prompted Alvarez.

'Oh, yeah, I for sure saw her again. She phoned the firm two days later and told 'em they could have the car back because hers had been repaired. So another bloke and me drove up to the village to collect the one-three-two. When we got to her place, she said her car didn't seem quite right after all and she'd hang on to the hire one for a few more days. That meant I had to return here for another insurance form and then drive back on my own for her signature. She gave me a drink by the pool and said I looked peaky and I ought to eat better than I obviously was. I wasn't arguing about that. She said why didn't I have supper with her that evening . . .' He looked at Carol, an expression of defiant pleading on his face: she was staring at the passing traffic.

'That evening she gave me a meal that had my guts getting in a frenzy just at the sight and smell of the grub: a couple of steaks the size of battleships, chips, onions, a plateful of cheese, ice-cream pudding hidden under whipped cream . . . I tell you, I should have made the *Guinness Book of Records* with what I ate that night.

'You're not going to believe this, but the penny hadn't dropped, not even then.' He balled his fists. He looked at Carol, but she was still staring out at the road. 'She said to go and see her again. I said sure, thanks, meaning I'd better things to do than spend the time with a middle-aged woman. But by the next evening I was so goddamn hungry that all I could think of was the meal I'd had the night before: trouble was, that had jerked me out of the habit of being hungry. I didn't go that night, but I did the next. She was all sugary and solicitous: been expecting me the previous night and had had the servants cook a chicken with roast potatoes—why hadn't I gone?

'She talked about my work. Why was I wasting my time as an ordinary mechanic? Why didn't I start up a business and run it efficiently so that I'd get all the work because the local firms were so inefficient and the staff off-hand? . . . Money, I said. She laughed. Money? How much did I need?

'I knew there was an opening because with the two firms there were then you were lucky if you got a car with four wheels. I spent several evenings working out the figures: I talked to a bloke I'd palled up with and he agreed to come in with me: I looked around and found a place that would do a treat: I had a chat with a Seat distributor and got him to agree to knock off an extra five per cent over the normal trade terms . . . It needed fifty thousand quid to get the business running. In two years it would be making a profit of seven thousand, even if the number of tourists didn't grow . . . I can tell you, I was bloody nervous about explaining to her I needed all of fifty thousand quid: for me, that sort of money was five fortunes. But she didn't bat an eyelid. Just said I needn't pay her back until everything was working really well . . . I've always wanted my own business. You're out there fighting for you, not for some load of fat-arsed directors or the government. It was like being told I'd won the pools . . . I'd forgotten something. I hadn't coughed up the stake money.'

Carol finally turned and looked at him. 'Stake money?'

His voice became contemptuous. 'When she first said to move into her place, I thought she was just being that much kinder. Offering me a home until I got the business moving and could rent or buy a decent flat . . . Then the truth finally sunk through my thick skull. If I was to get that business, she was to get herself a gigolo. I'm telling you, I was a bit shocked! But If I hadn't been so bloody dumb, I'd have seen it from the beginning.'

'Or if you had not been pursuing a dream,' said Alvarez.

'Why d'you say that?' he asked, surprised.

'Señor, when one wants something very much one often fails to see what lies on either side.'

'George,' said Carol, 'why have you been so ashamed of what happened? At first you'd no idea of what she really wanted, but as soon as you did you refused to have anything more to do with her.'

'No,' he said harshly.

She was suddenly afraid.

'I'll tell you what I did. I looked at the swimming pool, the house, and the garden: I thought about the booze and the grub . . . I remembered my digs, scruffy and dismal even in midsummer . . . And I thought about the fifty thousand quid and how if I worked all hours God made I'd surely turn the business into a really profitable one . . . And I wondered how I could be such a bloody fool as to think of refusing to move in with her.'

'But you did refuse,' said Alvarez, making it a statement of fact.

'In the end. But what makes me so bloody ashamed is that it took so long to decide.'

Carol reached across to put her hand on his.

Alvarez said: 'It is easy to be pompous in such matters, but when a man is offered strong temptations it does take much courage to resist them. That it needs time to become courageous is to be expected.' He signalled to a passing waiter. 'You refused a drink before but I think that perhaps now you will have one?'

Trent nodded. He was a very proud man and his confession had hurt: but to his astonishment he was discovering that with the hurt came a measure of absolution.

The waiter took their orders and went inside.

'Señor, there is one more thing I need to know. Why did the señora in her will leave you the pewter cigarette case?'

'I've told you all I can. I've never seen it before.'

'I was hoping that you really knew, but had not wished to speak before . . . If it had been made of gold, one could say it was an expression of her admiration for your courage.'

'And one would be hopelessly wrong.'

'In what way?'

'There's a saying about not being unkind to the dead, but where she's concerned that's asking too much. She'd never forgive anyone who balked her: if you didn't do as she wanted, she hated your guts, now and for evermore.'

The waiter returned and put three glasses down on the table. They drank.

'Perhaps,' said Alvarez slowly, 'it was after all a small token of her feelings, but not as I have previously presented it: perhaps it was an expression of hatred, not admiration. Yet why bother to express such hatred in so hidden and roundabout a way?' Then, abruptly, he remembered the scratches on the locks of the desk in the study, almost certainly made by Erington when reading through her private papers and stealing money. If she had been as smart and as hard as Trent presented her, might she not have discovered that her money was being stolen and that her papers were being read? Might she not have set out to threaten Erington, without his realizing he was being threatened? Knowing he would read it, a will drawn up by the local solicitor instead of her Palma one—because she needed it in a hurry—under the terms of which the whole of her fortune was to be his if he were faithful to her. But the equivalent of a battered pewter cigarette case if he were stupid enough to betray her . . . 'Señor, can you tell me something? Is Señor Erington friendly with a young lady who lives on this island?'

Carol and Trent looked at each other, their expressions similar. Alvarez, therefore, was not surprised when Trent said, in a harsh voice: 'He's been out with Carol.'

'Recently?'

'Yes,' said Carol.

'And did the señora know this?'

Trent shrugged his shoulders. 'God knows. But in this place nothing's private.'

'I think we may assume the señora had heard rumours . . . Señorita, have you been out with him very often?'

'Only once, really. George didn't like my seeing him, but I was . . . Well, in some ways I was sorry for him. And anyway, when he wasn't with Dolly he was good company.' She said to Trent: 'You don't have to tell me what you're thinking.'

Alvarez finished his drink. 'Thank you very much for your help.' He stood. 'And please do not worry about certain other matters we briefly discussed: I am old enough to have a very poor memory at times.'

CHAPTER 17

Victoriana opened the front door of Ca Na Nadana and as Alvarez entered, she said: 'He's in the pool, having a swim.' The tenor of her voice told him that she had begun to wonder what it would be like to be the señora of this luxury villa.

He walked through the sitting-room and round the house patio to the pool patio. Erington waved before swimming three lengths of the pool, cutting through the water with a stylish, powerful crawl. Then, disdaining to return to the steps at the shallow end, he reached up to the coping stone and hauled himself out with lithe grace. Done to impress? Alvarez wasn't certain. He only knew for sure that if he'd tried to swim one length of the pool at speed and then haul himself out like that, he'd have suffered a coronary thrombosis.

' 'Morning,' said Erington. 'Fantastic weather, isn't it? Already thirty-one in the shade so it'll be close on thirty-five by the early afternoon.'

Money made a man stand taller, thought Alvarez. 'Señor, whatever it is now, it is already too hot for work.'

'Then you're not here in your official capacity?'

'I am, but I am also too hot.'

'A couple of iced drinks will take care of that. I'll get Victoriana . . .'

'Perhaps we might first talk?'

'Business before pleasure? OK, if that's the way it's got to be. Let's move to the shade.'

They walked to the covered patio. Chairs were set out round the glass-topped table and they sat, Erington placing a folded towel on his chair beforehand.

'Señor, will you please tell me when you travelled to England and when you came back?'

'Left on Thursday and returned on Monday.'

'Did you return to this island between those days?'

'Did I what? . . . Good God, of course I didn't!'

'Have you someone who can verify that?'

'How d'you mean?'

'Is there someone in England who will be able to say exactly where you were Saturday night and early Sunday morning?'

Erington picked up the gold case which lay on top of the table, opened it, offered Alvarez a cigarette, then helped himself to one. He flicked open the gold lighter. 'I'd have to be dumb not to see the real significance of that question.' He held the lighter out for Alvarez. 'You can really think it's possible I might have killed Dolly?'

'It is my job to question everyone, however unnecessary that may appear to be.'

'A diplomatically untruthful answer . . . Yes, there is someone who can vouch for my every movement from midday Saturday onwards.'

'May I have the name, please?'

'No.'

Alvarez waited patiently.

'Perhaps I'd better try to explain a little . . . Look, there are some situations which can rather embarrass a bloke . . .' He stopped, tapped the ash from his cigarette, then said: 'If I promise you that who I was with can have absolutely nothing to do with what happened to Dolly, will you accept that assurance?'

'I am afraid that I must have the person's name.'

'But . . . Hell! If the news got around, the local gossips would have a field day.'

'I do not understand.'

'You would the moment you knew the name of the lady.'

'You spent that time with a lady?'

Erington stared out across the garden. 'It's ironic, isn't it? When you're young, you're taught that if ever you do anything wrong, you'll inevitably be found out. Then you start to grow up and discover that that is a load of cod's, broadcast by long-suffering adults who want some peace and quiet. Finally, you finish growing up and you learn that it's so often true . . .' He stubbed out the cigarette. 'I was with Samantha Waite. Her maiden name was Lund. She's Dolly Lund's daughter.'

Alvarez entered his office, switched on the fan, crossed to the chair behind the desk and slumped down on to it. The heat, even with closed shutters and the fan on, was stifling. Eventually, sweating from the effort, he reached out to the telephone and dialled Superior Chief Salas's number. Señor Salas, reported his superior secretary, was out. Hardly believing his luck, he explained what he wanted. Erington claimed that from Saturday afternoon to Monday morning he had been staying with Samantha

Waite, daughter of Señora Lund: her address, Flat 3a, Pemsbury Road, Hanwell, London. Could a request be forwarded to the English police to question Señora Waite about his alibi? And could this request be accompanied by a note that it seemed certain Erington had returned to Mallorca over Saturday night and early Sunday morning?

He rang the immigration department in Palma. It was necessary for every immigration card, handed in between 0000 hours Saturday morning and 2400 hours Sunday night to be checked and for a list of all men who had not been travelling with a family to be drawn up.

Finally, he telephoned Palma CID. He wanted all car hire firms in Palma to be interviewed and a list made of men who had hired a car between 0000 hours Saturday and 2400 hours Sunday.

He replaced the receiver, relaxed, and closed his eyes. It was pleasant to contemplate the lot of all the people who were going to have to work on his behalf in the stifling heat . . .

Victoriana walked out to the pool and spoke to Erington, who lay sunbathing. 'Can me and Ana still have a swim?'

'Of course you can. Any time, just so long as there aren't any guests around.'

'Then maybe I'll have one now. I'm so hot.' She giggled. 'I've bought a new costume, but I don't know whether I dare wear it.'

'Scared of suffering from exposure?'

'There truly is so little of it. And the bits come undone so easily . . .'

'Bring me a nail file in case one of 'em sticks.'

He watched her return into the house. She didn't realize it yet, but she was going to be right out of luck. He wasn't wasting everything he'd gained on a village girl who in ten years' time would look as sexy as a sixty-five-year-old grandmother from Bootle.

She returned, clothed in two minute scraps of coloured cloth, precariously held together by tapes. She looked nervously out at the surrounding land, fearful one of the neighbours would see her and report her shame to her parents, in Inca. She went down the steps into the pool and splashed around, occasionally reaching up to make certain everything was still in place. 'I've brought my nail file,' she called out.

'I'll be with you in a minute.' He turned over on to his back and then brought the edge of the towel over his eyes to protect them from the sun. That visit from the local detective had shaken him more than he cared to admit. After all, it was little more than two days since Dolly had been found dead and yet already he was obviously suspected. Thank God he'd not been stupid enough to believe he could never be suspected and so had planned how to prevent that suspicion turning into certainty.

There was more splashing from the pool, reminding him that she was waiting for him to join her. He'd have to get rid of her. He was no good at resisting temptation.

At dawn on Wednesday there were some clouds, the first for days, and a hint of mist which clung to the slopes of the hills and mountains and blurred their outlines. Then the sun rose to dismiss the clouds and burn away the mist, exposing both hills and mountains in all their starkness.

The heat increased, stifling the land. Those Mallorquins who had to be out in the sun covered themselves up and moved slowly and carefully: the tourists who had paid to be out in it stripped off and sunbathed without heed to their burning skins.

The phone-call from Superior Chief Salas's office came through at a quarter to twelve, as Alvarez sat in his office and thought how worn out he felt. 'We've heard from England. Señora Waite says she first met Erington last year. She liked him then and saw quite a bit of him. She knew he was her mother's gigolo, but she's broad-minded. She kept having rows with her mother, because of her independent attitude, and these became worse when her husband deserted her and she needed financial help. Her mother refused to help directly, so she wrote to Erington, begging him to do what he could for her. He tried to talk her mother round and then invented his own mother's illness as the excuse to fly back to England to see her. He told her that for the moment there was no chance her mother would relent and help her financially, but he was certain that given time and if she kept a low profile and he did all he could on her behalf, eventually Señora Lund would rally round.

'Despite all he said Señora Waite remained so depressed he had to cheer her up and one thing led to another and pretty soon they discovered they both liked bed. He stayed in her flat from Saturday afternoon to early Monday morning, when he left to get his plane back to this island . . . You know something? If anyone asks me, there's a touch of incest about the relationship!'

The two further reports arrived within half an hour of each other, late the same afternoon. Immigration supplied a list of one hundred and seventy-three names — accompanying this was a bad-tempered note pointing out the work that had been involved. Palma CID supplied a list of forty-two names. Alvarez compared the two and after a long and boring task discovered that no one name appeared on both lists.

He stared at the shuttered window. Of course, Erington might have been travelling with a false passport in one name and a driving licence in another. But that would be to take an obvious risk because there was always the chance that a car hire firm would demand to see both passport and licence. The elaborate planning of this murder suggested someone who would never have taken an obvious risk . . . In any case, didn't Señora Waite say he had been with her during the relevant time . . .

He leaned back in the chair, sweating, thirsty, tired, and defeated.

CHAPTER 18

Alvarez drove slowly through the narrow streets, many without pavements, so that pedestrians were a constant hazard, and parked in the square because there was no room closer to the guardia post. He climbed out, blinked at the harsh sunshine, and walked towards the road which led down to the post. His route—which could not by any stretch of the imagination be called direct—happened to bring him close to the main entrance of the Club Llueso. Gratefully he went into the bar, ordered a coffee and a brandy, and then sat at one of the window tables.

As he watched the people outside—many of them tourists who seemed in a perpetual hurry—he thought gloomily that it was an open and shut case in which everything opened and nothing shut. After all, who but Erington could repeatedly have forced the locks on the desk in the study and read the papers inside? Who else could so easily have procured a key to let himself into the house to murder while making the death appear an accident (which it would have done if only he hadn't made the mistake of removing too many pills from a bottle which had obviously only just been opened)? Who else knew so certainly that Señora Lund would be too drunk to struggle, or even aware of what was going on, that only Victoriana would be in the house and that she could hear very little from her room . . .

Damnit, if there were no one else—there had been no suggestion of any motive other than the money—then he had to be right. Which meant that the mistake was not in naming Erington the murderer, but in accepting that the evidence proved he was not. So where was that mistake . . .

Erington was a cunning man: weak but cunning. He had planned the murder very carefully. So wouldn't he have visualized the possibility of the death being identified as murder and have envisaged the need to give himself an alibi . . .

He poured the brandy into the coffee. If only he were clever, could think more clearly, then it would all become obvious. But his thoughts forever muddled into each other, cannoning off to disappear without trace . . . He swore. Wasn't the solution obvious, even to a dolt, from the moment one accepted that Erington had to be the murderer and the mistake was in the evidence which proved he was not?

Alvarez spoke to Salas over the phone. 'Señor, I am aware that England has reported that Señora Waite says that Erington was with her throughout Saturday night. But if one accepts that Erington must be the murderer, then she had to be lying.

'A remark made to me on the relationship between Erington and Señora Waite has been troubling me. It was described as being like incest. Does that not suggest something?'

'It suggests a diseased mind. What in the devil are you talking about?'

'I find it very difficult to express my thoughts, señor. But this is what I am trying to say. Señora Waite knew that Erington was her mother's gigolo. How would any daughter view such a relationship? With distaste. And in this particular case, wouldn't this distaste be transferred into hatred because the daughter would seize the opportunity of blaming the gigolo for the estrangement between her mother and herself? She would never take the man she hated as her lover.'

'Am I to congratulate you or Freud on so masterly a diagnosis?'

'Señor, all I can say is, that is how a woman of the soil would think.'

'I must, of necessity, take your word for that.'

'But I am sure it is so.'

'What if it is?'

'Then I think that the Señora Waite who lives in the flat in London is not the real Señora Waite.'

'The English police interviewed her—they would have made certain of her identity.'

'To what extent? We didn't ask them to verify that she was Señora Waite. We merely asked them to interview the Señora Waite who lived in the flat. And in England, I believe, people do not have to carry identity papers. Don't you see, señor, that if Erington is as clever as I believe, he will have prepared for the need to have an alibi which can be verified.'

'You are overlooking the fact that that raises the risk the police might easily have interviewed the true Señora Waite.'

'Not easily. There unfortunately was very bad feeling between the mother and the daughter. There is in Ca Na Nadana part of the draft of a letter which Señora Lund wrote to her daughter. It makes a man tremble to think there can be such maternal wickedness . . .'

'It will be very much quicker for both of us if you cut out the moralizing.'

'Of course . . . Suppose the mother and daughter were on such bad terms that the daughter did not even know where her mother now lived: that she did not even care where she now lived and had sworn never again to try to get in touch with her? Then what are the chances of the real daughter's present whereabouts accidentally coming to light?'

There was a short pause. 'What do you propose?'

'With your permission, I will ask England to check the identity of the woman in the flat. And for that I can supply them with a photograph of Señora Waite and a holographic letter, written by her recently . . . When it is obvious she is not Señora Waite, we will have the final proof that Erington is the murderer.'

CHAPTER 19

Detective-Constable Flynn braked the Escort to a stop. 'Here we are, then: Pemsbury Road. A year or so back we picked up Shorty Mason in one of the houses further along this road.'

'Who?' asked PC Questead, recently attached to CID as an aide.

'You don't know Shorty? Where were you transferred from—Caithness?'

'Kew.'

Flynn grinned. 'From under the river, from the sound of it.'

They left the car, crossed the pavement, and climbed the six stone steps up to the front door of the large, ugly Victorian house. To the right of the door were a number of bell pushes, each tagged with a name, and a speaker unit. Questead pressed the button for flat 3a. A woman's voice, rendered tinny by the speaker, said: 'Who is it?'

'Local CID, Mrs Waite. Could we have a word with you?'

'Again?'

' 'Fraid so. Only it was someone else last time.'

'I suppose you'd better come up.'

There was a quick buzz from the door and when they pushed, it opened.

'Don't forget,' said Flynn, 'if she's half as snappy as the photo, leave me to do the talking.'

They entered the hall and climbed the uncarpeted stairs, their shoes thumping on the wooden treads. There were four flats on the third, and top, floor and 3a was nearest to the head of the stairs on the left. The door was opened by a blonde in her middle twenties. She had an oval face with high cheekbones, blue eyes, a pert nose, and a well curved mouth with full, moist lips. Plenty of sex appeal, not too discreetly handled. The top button on her flowered housecoat was undone. Flynn smiled his smoothest smile as they stepped into the bedsitting-room. 'Sorry to bust in on you like this, Mrs Waite, only we have to check up on a couple of facts.'

She spoke petulantly. 'I was about to get into the bath when you rang. I hope you won't be long: I'm meeting someone for lunch.'

Flynn visualized what she was not wearing under the housecoat. 'Won't take any time at all. And in fact, our first question's already answered.'

'What are you on about?'

He took the photograph from his inside coat pocket. 'We're here to make certain you're you, if you see what I mean.' He tapped the photograph. 'There couldn't be two of you so alike: not both that beautiful.'

You're overdoing it, thought Questead dispassionately.

'Let's have a look at that.' She was handed the photograph. 'Of course that's me. It was taken just before Paul . . .' She stopped, turned, and went over to a small table and picked up a pack of cigarettes. 'Either of you smoke?'

'Like a chimney,' answered Flynn, accepting a cigarette.

'Thanks all the same, but I don't,' said Questead.

'Nuts on physical fitness and all that jazz,' said Flynn, indicating the PC with a supercilious nod of his head. He struck a match for her and as she leaned forward to light her cigarette he looked down the front of her housecoat.

She straightened up, handed him back the photograph, then sat on one of the battered easy chairs.

'Last thing is,' said Flynn, 'would you mind writing a bit for us?'

'Yes, I would, unless you explain a bit more what all this is in aid of.'

'It's on account of Spain, Mrs Waite. You know what odd-balls foreigners are. They've asked us to make certain you really are Mrs Lund's daughter.'

'What's it matter if I am or not? She didn't give a damn.'

'Something to do with the will, maybe.'

'She told me months and months ago she wouldn't leave me anything. When I was so ill and asked her for help, she even refused . . .' She became silent.

'Sorry about all that, love. A bit of cash to leave, was there?'

'Enough that if it had come to me I wouldn't ever again have had to worry about paying the bills.'

'Makes it extra rough . . . D'you think you could help us now and find a pen and paper?'

She shrugged her shoulders, stood, and walked out of the room. Flynn turned and winked at Questead, who merely nodded. Didn't recognize a hot wicket when he met one, thought Flynn scornfully.

She returned with a ballpoint pen and a pad of notepaper. She sat, careful this time to smooth down the housecoat, rested the pad on her knees, and said: 'What d'you want me to write, then?'

'I'll dictate a bit, if that's all right with you.' He took the facsimile of one of the letters from his coat pocket and slowly began to read out.

She stopped writing and looked up. 'That's from one of my letters, isn't it?' Her voice was tight.

'It could be.'

'What right have you to have it? Who said you could poke and pry into our private affairs?'

'Sorry, love, but straight it's nothing to do with us this end. We're only carrying out what the Spanish police have asked us to.'

'Oh God, why do I have to be dragged through all this after what's happened?'

'Just a little more,' coaxed Flynn. He read out three short sentences. 'That's that. Let's have what you've written, can I?'

She tore the page out of the pad and handed it to him.

'Very many thanks for all your help, Mrs Waite.'

She did up the top button of her housecoat.

As they made their way downstairs, Questead said: 'Was the handwriting the same?'

'Exactly . . . Lovely bit of crackling, eh?'

'But went a bit cold on you.'

Miserable bastard, thought Flynn.

Dolores put the earthenware bowl of soup on the dining table, by the side of the basket of oven-dried thinly sliced bread.

'Caldereta!' said Jaime enthusiastically.

She stared at Alvarez and saw that his attention was far away: a look of annoyance spread over her handsome, regal face. 'Perhaps some people expected something far better?'

'Hurry up, Mum,' said Juan, with all the impatience of a starving eleven-year-old.

Jaime kicked Alvarez under the table.

'God Almighty!' Alvarez exclaimed, as he leaned over to rub his shin.

'Wake up, Uncle,' said Juan delightedly.

'Do you want some soup?' asked Isabel.

'Anything that's going.'

'Get your uncle a slice of bread and some cheese,' said Dolores, with disdain.

Very belatedly, Alvarez realized what the trouble was. 'Caldereta! Wonderful!'

Jaime chuckled. 'Three parts asleep. Spent the afternoon with the widow along the road, I suppose.'

'Jaime!' snapped Dolores.

'Only joking.'

She served, putting three slices of bread into each plate and then ladling the fish soup over it.

The telephone rang as Dolores, helped by Isabel, was clearing away the soup plates. Alvarez answered it.

'London's just been through to us, Enrique,' said one of the guards from the post. 'They confirm that the woman in the flat is Señora Waite.'

'Confirm? . . . But she can't be.'

'That's what the message said.'

'I tell you, it's impossible.'

'Argue it out with them, mate, not me.'

The guard said a brief goodbye and cut the connection. Alvarez stared blankly at the wall, the receiver still in his hand.

'Are you coming back,' Dolores called out, 'or shall I keep your food warm?'

He returned to the dining-room and sat.

'You look as if that was bad news,' she said, suddenly worried.

'It's going to be very bad news when I report it tomorrow morning to Salas.'

Jaime pushed a bottle of wine across the table. 'Tomorrow's tomorrow. Drink and enjoy what's left of today.'

CHAPTER 20

In his office, Alvarez replaced the telephone receiver.
There had not been any need for Salas to have been quite
so sarcastic: every man made mistakes at some stage of his
career, even the Salases of the world.

He stared through the unshuttered window at the sun-
blasted wall of the house on the opposite side of the road.
So the woman in the flat *was* Señora Waite: she *had*
received Erington in her bed, even though she knew him
to be her mother's gigolo: Erington *had* been in England
throughout Saturday night and Sunday morning and so
he had not murdered Señora Lund.

He lit a cigarette. Erington wasn't the murderer, so
who was? Who else had the motive, the opportunity, the
will to murder . . . ? Matas? Or the señor who, according
to Victoriana, had borrowed money from the señora and
had then been asked to pay a wicked amount of interest
which he couldn't afford? Or Trent, who had proudly
refused to be her gigolo? . . . Even if one accepted that
murder could be committed for slight motives, was it
really reasonable to believe that any of those motives
could have been sufficient?

What had he been taught all those long and only
half-remembered years ago in Barcelona? In every
crime, look to the motive: motive identifies the criminal
as surely as his fingerprint. When there were hundreds
of millions of pesetas at stake, how could the motive
be anything but the money? Yet only Erington inherited . . .

Dear God, a man could destroy his brain by too much
worrying. Forget it.

He stared at the tangle of papers on his desk and

thought that he really ought to start work on them. But not just yet . . .

Alvarez had had to speak to a man down in the Port and he was driving back to Llueso when, for no immediately discernible reason, he suddenly remembered something Victoriana had said to him. 'Looks quite nice now, doesn't she?' At the time it had meant nothing. But now . . . ?

He carried on past the football ground and turned right on to the Festona road, slowed for the dirt track, and bounced over the pot holes to Ca Na Nadana.

Ana opened the front door and he asked if Victoriana was in? 'She's still here, yes, but she'll be leaving later on. The señor says he only needs one of us to run the house now it's just him living here.' It was impossible to judge from her manner how she felt about this.

'I want a word with her. And is the señor here?'

'He drove into Palma earlier on.'

He went into the sitting-room and several seconds later there were several short, sharp yaps as Lulu reached the doorway through which he'd just passed. She waddled across to sniff his trousers. Eventually recognizing him, she wagged her tail. He bent down and stroked her.

Victoriana, dressed in a brilliantly coloured frock, walked into the room.

'Good morning, señorita. I hear you are leaving here?'

'Kicked out, just like that,' she answered bitterly. 'Been working here for nearly three years, but that doesn't mean anything to him. These foreigners all think they can treat us like slaves.'

'After three years, surely he can't dismiss you just like that? Not with the law on employment as it is now.'

She looked slyly resentful. 'Well, he did give me a bit of cash. But with all his money and after three years, you'd have thought he'd have made it more.'

It was easy to judge that what she really resented was Erington's refusal to consider marrying her. 'Señorita, I have to check something with you. Do you remember the first day I came to this house: just after you'd found the señora dead?'

'Not likely to forget that in a hurry, am I? Keep having nightmares of finding her dead again.'

'I asked you a lot of questions, one of which was about the photo of her daughter which was on the dressing-table in her bedroom.'

'Did you?'

'I wanted to know if the woman in the photo was the señora's daughter. You said yes, she was, and didn't she look quite nice now . . . What made you say that?'

'Why shouldn't I?'

'It's the "now" I'm interested in.'

'I don't get you.'

'Señorita, why did you say "now", as if some time previously things had been different? Hadn't the daughter always looked nice?'

'Not before, she didn't. Every time I looked, I thought what a bad-tempered, spoiled kid she must have been.'

'Every time you looked at what? A different photo? One taken when the daughter was much younger?'

'That's what I've just said, isn't it?'

'How old d'you think she was in the other photo?' he asked, with endless patience.

She shrugged her shoulders. 'I don't know. Ten, maybe.'

'And when was that photo changed: recently?'

'Yeah.'

'How recently?'

'Can't rightly say. When something's always there, you don't really notice it, do you?'

'Then when was it that you first realized the photo had been changed?'

She thought back. 'Can't really remember seeing it before the Sunday. I opened the curtains and pushed the shutters back and turned and noticed the different photo before looking at her to see if she was awake . . .' She became silent.

He ought to have realized the significance of the photo very much sooner: a clever man would certainly have done so. The señora had disinherited her daughter: in those circumstances, was it likely she would ever have replaced a photo of her daughter when young and still under her dominion with one taken when her daughter had become antagonistically independent? . . . Erington had changed the photos.

And because one key had turned and opened one lock, now another turned to open a second one. Those letters from Samantha to her mother. Two envelopes had been crumpled but the sheets of papers inside had not been: the dates of three of the letters had not matched the postmarks of the envelopes. At the time, sentimentally he had projected a sentimental reason for the facts . . . Even to tear drops . . . But now, with hindsight, he could see design, not sentiment. The envelopes, containing something unimportant, perhaps advertising material, had been sent to the señora: two of them had been crumpled up and thrown away by her before Erington had been able to retrieve them. The letters to go inside the envelopes had been sent to Erington and in three cases the writer had forgotten to correlate the dates. The reason for all this? So that Dolly Lund's fingerprints would be on the envelopes to prove she had handled them. (A totally wasted precaution because a slow-witted inspector in the Cuerpo General de Policia had never stopped to doubt that she had!) The woman who had written and posted the letters, which were to verify her own identity, was the woman who had been living as Samantha Waite in London. Because Erington was a clever man, he had foreseen the possibility that doubts would be cast on her identity and so he had provided the proof of the lie . . .

'Is there anything more you want?' asked Victoriana impatiently.

He started. 'What's that?'

'I've got to catch the bus to Inca and time's getting on. If I miss this one, I'll have to hang around for hours and the sooner I get clear of this place, the better I'll like it.'

'Of course, señorita. I'm sorry to have taken up your time. But just before you go, I need your home address.'

After she had left the room, he walked over to one of the windows and stared out at the kidney-shaped swimming pool, doubly inviting in the brilliant sunshine. All right, the woman in flat 3a was a fraud. But that still left one very important question unanswered. How had Erington managed to fly to the island, drive from Palma to Llueso and back again, and fly to London, all without leaving the slightest trace of his passing? Why hadn't Carolina Cardell, suffering from toothache, heard a car go past since she'd been awake for much of the night? Of course she could have slept more often and for longer than she thought, but wouldn't the passing of a car have awakened someone sleeping so fitfully? . . . Only the Mobylette had passed at about two in the morning. (That prompted the thought that he'd never checked up to make certain whether the bike had been ridden by one of the four people with land further up the track. But unless one of them had an animal ill—and then the old couple would surely have known about it—it was difficult to accept that it could have been any of them.) Could Erington have been riding the Mobylette? Palma to Llueso and back was about a hundred and ten kilometres and that was far too long a journey for such a vehicle. In any case, the bike had returned along the track only half an hour afterwards, one and a half hours before the estimated time of death . . .

Suppose he had been Erington, planning this murder. Then obviously, knowing how essential it was that no one recognized him, the entire journey became dangerous. A fellow passenger on either plane might live in Llueso. There were always couriers at the airport, waiting for incoming flights or seeing off passengers on outgoing ones, and several couriers lived in either Llueso or Puerto Llueso . . . The odds against arriving and departing without being seen were really too great to be risked . . .

He suddenly swore aloud. God had granted him few brains, but at least he might have used those which he had been given. Ca Na Nadana was six kilometres from the Port and what easier than to ride up from there on one of the very small motorized bikes which many boats carried . . .

Now it was all so obvious that the only point of mystery was how it could have taken him so long to discover the truth. Erington had flown from London to Menorca, where no one knew him. He had set sail in a motor yacht, previously chartered, and had crossed to Mallorca, specifically Puerto Llueso, a voyage which might have taken under two hours. He'd anchored in the bay, gone ashore in the tender, taking the motorized bike with him, and ridden the bike from the Port to Ca Na Nadana, passing the old couple's home just after two. (The doctor, annoyed this was necessary because he was a man of much precision, had warned against accepting his estimate of the time of death.) He'd used a key to enter the house, had gone upstairs and had murdered Dolly Lund. He'd returned to the Port, set sail for Menorca, flown to London . . .

So now there were more facts which had to be checked. Who had recently chartered a fast motor yacht in Menorca? Had the harbourmasters of either Ciudadela or Puerto Llueso noted the passage of the yacht . . .

.

At six-forty-eight on Monday evening, Erington replaced the telephone in the hall of Ca Na Nadana and swore. Carol had said she was very sorry, but she wasn't free tonight. Nor tomorrow night. She'd been lying. Refusing to go out with him because she believed the rumours, which must inevitably be circulating, that it had been he who had murdered Dolly? He shook his head. She would never think the worst of anyone until circumstances positively forced her to do so—it was this stubborn belief in goodness which had always so attracted him. Then the reason had to be that she had become too friendly with Trent. Which was absurd. A mechanic, straight from the slums, when he could offer her wealth untold . . .

He walked through the sitting-room to the patio. Wasn't he really a fool to bother with her any more? When she walked into a restaurant, no heads would turn. Her natural milieu was a semi-detached in Tonbridge, not the Pink Suite in the Parelona Hotel. Now that he was no longer a middle-aged woman's impecunious gigolo, but was rich, surely he was not going to be a fool to search for something he no longer needed?

Ana walked out on to the patio. 'There is a señor who wishes to speak to you.'

She amused him. Now that Victoriana had left, she had become even more reserved than before. Did she fear that one night he'd try to break into her bedroom? . . . She could always allay such fears by looking at a mirror. 'Who is it?'

'Inspector Alvarez.'

He sighed as he sat. 'Like the bad penny, always turning up . . . OK, bring him out here. And since he's a thirsty type, wheel out the drinks.' He lit a cigarette as she returned indoors. How much longer before the bungling detective finally managed to put two and two together and accepted that the evidence proved he'd had nothing to do with Dolly's death?

When Alvarez came out of the house, he nodded and said hullo, but did not bother to get to his feet and shake hands. He was rich now.

'Señor, with your permission I have a few questions.'

'Heaven only knows how you can dredge up any more . . . Grab a seat. There's no extra charge for sitting.' As Alvarez settled, he said: 'What is it this time? What did I have for breakfast a week ago?'

'No, señor. When were you last in Menorca?'

The question shocked him and his previous thoughts returned to mock him: how much longer before the bumbling detective managed to put two and two together? He gained time by offering cigarettes and then lighting them. 'The only time I've been on that island is something around a year ago. Dolly, in a rare burst of enthusiasm, decided she wanted to explore Menorca, so we booked a hotel for three days and went over in the morning with our car on the ferry from Playa Neuva. By the end of the afternoon we'd been everywhere and seen everything, so we returned that same evening.'

'Did you not fly to Menorca from London a week ago last Saturday?'

'I most certainly did not.'

'And did you not hire a car from Hertz at Mahon airport and drive to Ciudadela?'

Erington felt an icy cold settle in his stomach, yet the sweat was breaking out on his forehead and his body.

'And did you not sail from Cuidadela in a motor yacht called *Pariki Three* which you had earlier chartered, by telephone, for a fortnight?'

He struggled to overcome the fog of panic and gratefully saw Ana wheel out the cocktail cabinet. After she had told them there were stuffed olives, toasted almonds and ice on the top shelf, he spent a long time putting the small earthenware bowls of olives and almonds on the glass-topped table and pouring out the drinks. Despite the time he took, Alvarez showed no signs of impatience. Like a bloody cow chewing the cud, he thought, knowing that his contempt was really fear.

Alvarez drank, put his glass down on the table. 'Señor, it will be much easier for everyone, including yourself, if you now tell me the truth about where you were and what you did on the night of the seventeenth and the early morning of the eighteenth.'

'I've told you. If you won't believe me, get on to Samantha Waite . . .'

'She has already been questioned twice, but because there is still doubt the English police have been requested to question her very closely a third time and to ask her to prove—without the aid of letters she had previously written or a photograph of herself—that she really is the daughter of Señora Lund.'

Erington finished his drink and poured himself another. Momentarily, his fear was submerged by a wild, unreasoning anger—how could this dolt of a man have had the incredible luck to stumble on the truth? 'I can tell you one thing for absolute certain—you've got a wild imagination. The English police can question Samantha until they're blue in the face and all they'll discover is that she's Dolly's daughter.'

Alvarez spoke curiously. 'Did it not occur to you that no daughter would ever wish her mother's gigolo to make love to her?'

'It didn't occur to me because it happened.'

'Señor, you are perhaps a very clever man, but I do not think you understand much about people . . . On the seventeenth you flew from Gatwick to Mahon under the name of Brown: you arrived at eight-forty-five. You hired a car from Hertz, at the airport, also in the name of Brown, and you drove to Ciudadela, where you boarded a motor yacht called *Pariki Three* which you had previously chartered. On this yacht there was a large inflatable, with an outboard, and a small motorized bike, of the kind which is very popular on boats. You sailed from Ciudadela and arrived at Puerto Llueso just after a quarter to one on Sunday morning. You did not enter the harbour, but anchored in the bay and went ashore in the inflatable, taking the bike with you. You rode from the port to here and passed the caseta at the beginning of the dirt track just after two o'clock. You murdered the señora by asphyxiating her with a pillow. You rode back to the Port, sailed to Ciudadela, drove to Mahon, and caught a plane back to Gatwick which left at ten-fifteen in the morning.'

'I didn't kill her,' said Erington violently. 'I was in London all the time. Can't you understand, I was in London.'

'I have spoken by phone to the immigration officials at Mahon airport, to the clerk who was on duty at the Hertz desk, to the firm which chartered the yacht. There are many men who will be able to identify you as Brown.'

'I was in London,' he shouted, as if to reiterate the lie more and more forcibly would be to turn it into the truth.

'Then together we must go to Menorca to discover what all these people say. You will please not travel further on this island than the village until we have been to Menorca and you will now bring me your passport. Should you consider leaving under the name of Brown, using the passport you have used before, I must warn you that all officials on this island have been alerted to that possibility.'

Erington stood slowly, scared that his legs would no longer support him.

Alvarez awoke, stared up at the ceiling, and thought that when he telephoned Superior Chief Salas he would try to display due humility when he announced that events had proved him right after all.

The phone downstairs rang. There was a shout from Dolores that the call was for him.

He put on a thin cotton dressing-gown over his pyjama trousers and went downstairs. 'Enrique, guardia post here. You'd better get along to Ca Na Nadana bloody quick. There's another corpse.'

CHAPTER 21

Alvarez parked in the drive of Ca Na Nadana, crossed to the front door, and was about to ring the bell when the door was opened by Ana. Her face was white and drawn and she was trembling. 'It's ghastly . . . Mother of God, it's ghastly . . .'

He put a comforting arm around her shoulders, as a father would have done, and led her into the sitting-room, still in half dark because all the shutters were closed and curtains drawn, made her sit down. He saw the cocktail cabinet and went over and poured out a brandy. 'Get this down you,' he said, as he handed her the glass. 'I'm just going upstairs for a moment.'

He went up and along to Erington's room. The door was three parts open and he could see, in the half dark, that Erington lay sprawled diagonally across the bed on his back, his head nearest to the door. Alvarez went in. There was already a smell of death: in the heat, this quickly formed. Erington's eyes were closed and his mouth was slightly open so that his front teeth were just visible: ironically, his lips seemed to be smiling. There was a small wound on his forehead from which blood had flowed down the left-hand side of his scalp. By the corner of the bed, on the carpet, lay an automatic with so short a barrel that at first glance it seemed almost to be without one.

There was a sudden yap, which startled him so much he swore, and Lulu waddled into the room, stopping when just inside the doorway. Her bulging eyes seemed to be begging him to explain what was going on. He patted her head, fondled her ears, then called her out as he left.

Downstairs, he found that Ana had drunk half the brandy and was looking slightly less shocked. He sat beside her. 'Are you well enough now to tell me exactly what happened this morning, señorita?'

She nodded.

'Then as soon as you've told me, you must go to your home so that you can be with your family.'

A little colour had begun to creep into her thin cheeks and her trembling had slackened. 'I arrived here at eight,' she said, then stopped.

'Why were you arriving? Didn't you sleep here last night?'

'Yesterday, after you'd gone, he seemed all . . . all strange. Told me to go home, even though today wasn't my day off, because really he didn't need me . . . It just wasn't like him to be thoughtful and kind . . . I arrived here, like I said. Lulu was making a terrible noise upstairs, yapping. I went through to the kitchen to get things ready, but Lulu went on and on so I decided to find out what was up. She was in his room. I knocked, but there wasn't any answer, so I knocked again. Lulu began to howl and I opened the door just a little to let her out and called to ask him what he wanted for breakfast. There wasn't a sound, except that the air-conditioning was on and that was unusual because he always switched it off before he went to sleep. Then Lulu, she'd run to the stairs, came back and started howling once more and I suddenly thought . . . Well, I wondered if he'd suddenly been taken badly ill. So I pushed the door more open and looked inside . . .' She made a sound that was half moan, half a cry of horror.

'Did you go into the bedroom, señorita?'

'Go inside? . . . When he was there, sprawled all over the bed . . .'

He thought for a moment, then said: 'What doors have you unlocked and what shutters have you opened up since you've been here this morning?'

'I came into the house through the kitchen door.'

'Was it locked?'

'Of course it was.' She stared uneasily at him, as if he had asked a ridiculous question.

'And then?'

'I opened the shutters of the kitchen windows. I got the butter out of the fridge, because otherwise it's too solid to spread, prepared the coffee-machine, and then on account of Lulu yapping I went upstairs . . .'

'So the only shutters you've touched are the kitchen ones, and the only doors the kitchen and the front door, when you let me in. Was the front door locked?'

She nodded.

'Right. Now, would you like me to run you home or will you go back on whatever you came on?'

She hesitated, fiddled with a button on her dress, then said she'd return on her Mobylette.

After she had left, he checked the downstairs shutters and doors, accompanied most of the time by Lulu who seemed about to have hysterics. It suddenly occurred to him that she might want to go out and he opened the front door for her. He had been correct.

Upstairs, he went into Erington's room, shutting the door on Lulu. She marked her displeasure by giving brief yaps and scrabbling at the door. He unlatched the shutters of the nearest window and pushed them back until caught by the retaining clips. Sunlight speared into the room. It etched Erington's death in the starkest terms, where the previous dim light had almost confused it with sleep.

He looked around the room and saw the envelope, carefully propped up against one of two silver-backed brushes on the dressing-table. On the envelope were typed two words, 'The Police', in English. The flap was not sealed. The typed message inside, on a sheet of notepaper, was short and to the point. 'I can't face any more. I killed Dolly because I wanted her money.'

He returned the note into the envelope, crossed to the bed, and stared down at the dead man. What had been his thoughts and emotions just before he pulled the trigger? Remorse, relief because by his own death he was making some restitution, curiosity, or merely confused fear?

He left the room, patted Lulu, and went downstairs. He telephoned Dr Rosselló and as he was out left a message with his wife: the undertaker, to tell him to be ready to remove the body and to keep it in cold storage until further notice: and Superior Chief Salas.

'Señor, I am speaking from Ca Na Nadana, the house which belonged to Señora Lund.'

'Well?'

'It is now certain that I was correct in all that I surmised.' He paused, so that Salas could say something suitable. Salas said nothing. 'I spoke to Erington last night and confronted him with all the evidence I have collected: evidence which shows beyond doubt that he killed the señora and tried to set up an alibi by getting a woman to impersonate the señora's daughter. You will perhaps remember . . .'

'Could you try to be as brief as possible.'

'Very well, señor. This morning, Ana, who still works here, rang the police to say that she had discovered Erington's body in his bedroom. He was dead.'

'If there is a body it is surely normal for that person to be dead?'

'He had shot himself. He's left a note saying he intended to commit suicide and admitting to murdering the señora.'

'Then it would seem that not even you can confuse the issue.'

'Señor, I have said from the beginning that Erington . . .'

'You'll make a full report and send it to my office. And Alvarez . . .'

'Señor?'

'I want that report as soon as possible: not in six months' time.' He cut the connection.

A real man of Madrid, thought Alvarez with rare bitterness. Not a word of praise: not a hint of apology for ever having doubted: just arrogant indifference to anyone else's feelings.

He walked slowly through to the kitchen and saw two ensaimadas which had been put out on a plate, with some butter, on a tray, ready for Erington's breakfast. They decided him that he was hungry. The coffee-maker was on the stove: he lit the gas.

After eating the ensaimadas, shared with Lulu, and drinking two cups of coffee, he stacked the dirty plate and cup and saucer on the working surface near the washing-up machine and returned the butter to the fridge. The front doorbell rang.

Dr Rosselló proved to be in his usual hurry. 'Where is he?'

'Up in his bedroom, doctor: shot himself with an automatic. There's a suicide note . . .'

'Show me which room it is, please, and can't you stop that beastly little dog making such a frightful row?'

They went upstairs and Alvarez led the way into the bedroom. Rosselló put his small black bag down on a chair, clasped his hands behind his back, and studied the dead man.

Just like a little bantam cock, Alvarez thought, as he watched Rosselló move round the bed. Rosselló bent down and examined Erington's head more closely, at one point carefully parting the hair to reveal the scalp. 'No exit wound so the bullet's lodged somewhere inside.' He straightened up. 'Was he right- or left-handed?'

Alvarez thought. 'Right-handed.'

He brushed his moustache with crooked forefinger. 'Do you know what is meant by the classical sites of election in suicide by shooting?'

'I think so.'

'The right temple for right-handed people, left for left-handed, centre brow, roof of the mouth, and over the heart. This entry wound is on the left temple.'

'But presumably . . .'

'I am reasonably certain that this is not a contact wound and I would have expected more than just scattered tattooing.'

'You're not saying . . .' began Alvarez, a note of despair in his voice.

'I am saying nothing definite because only an expert can do that. But I am suggesting that this man did not shoot himself.'

CHAPTER 22

Alvarez seldom hated anyone, unless that person had inflicted physical or mental cruelty, because he was far too generous in his judgements, too ready to excuse, but as he watched Dr Rosselló drive away he hated the man. Before he had come to the house the case had been simple: now it was in danger of becoming desperately complicated.

He returned into the house. Perhaps, he thought with sudden hope, the experts would between them make nonsense of Rosselló's findings. After all, why shouldn't a right-handed man shoot himself in his left temple if he felt like it? . . . His hope dimmed. Rosselló was the kind of man who never spoke unless he was certain . . .

What was he going to say to Salas? he wondered as he entered the kitchen. He'd been so cocksure when he'd rung earlier that he hadn't left himself any room for backtracking . . . He crossed to the cupboard in which Victoriana had kept the bottle of Soberano containing Carlos I brandy and to his great relief found that it was still there. He half filled a tumbler and drank. After a while, life began to brighten up a little. Surely he was worrying over nothing? Erington had murdered Dolly Lund. Then if he now had been murdered, then, unless one believed in incredible coincidences, his murder was directly connected with hers. But since he was the sole person to benefit from her death . . .

He finished the brandy. For once, he thought, now almost cheerful, the precise Dr Rosselló had to be imprecisely wrong.

Alvarez crossed the square, ringed on two sides with plane trees whose leaves offered welcome shade, to the stall set in front of the church. He waited while a small boy was served with a strawberry cornet, then bought a cup of iced lemon. He sucked this through a couple of straws as he made his way slowly through the heat-sodden roads to the guardia post.

There was a message on his desk, telling him to ring the Institute of Forensic Anatomy.

'First of all,' said a cheerful-sounding man, 'tests have been completed on the stomach contents of the deceased, Señora Lund. These confirm that she had taken no sleeping pills within twenty-four hours of her death.

'Secondly, preliminary investigations into the death of Erington have shown that it was unlikely he shot himself, but that the possibility cannot be entirely ruled out. The site of the shooting is an unusual one for a right-handed person, but if the right hand is curled round the front of the head it is just possible to inflict such a wound. In this case, the maximum distance at which the gun could have been fired if taking note of the length of the deceased's right arm is just within the minimum distance at which the gun was fired according to the powder tattooing on the skin. Tests have been carried out on the deceased's hands for powder deposits, none has been found. Although this strongly suggests he had not fired the gun, once again the evidence is not conclusive: in some circumstances, these tests can fail to prove the negative, although they can always be accepted as proving the positive.'

'In a nutshell, you think he didn't commit suicide, but can't prove it?'

'That's the score exactly.'

Alvarez thanked the other and rang off. What were the odds against murder? Despite the forensic evidence, surely they remained high? What could possibly be the motive for the murder? On the known facts, only revenge or money. Dolly Lund's daughter might feel she had cause for revenge, but it seemed highly probable she didn't even yet know her mother was dead, almost certain she didn't know where her mother had been living or that she had been living with a gigolo. There'd hardly been time for Erington to double-cross the woman who'd played the part of Samantha Waite so why should she seek revenge? . . . Money? Had Erington made a will? Not that such a will would pass the money because no man was allowed to benefit from his own crime and therefore he could never have inherited Dolly's fortune.

But beyond all this lay two very important facts. First, the house had been locked up and there'd not been the slightest sign of a forced entry, so any intruder must have had a key. Someone else, beside Erington, who had a key to the house? Surely not. Second, if it had not been suicide, someone had set the scene to make it appear so: someone who knew that the evidence against Erington had suddenly become overwhelming. Who else but Erington and himself had known that? He had told no one until after Erington was murdered (that call to Salas!).Erington was hardly likely to have passed on the news . . .

It had been suicide. But with a last piece of incompetence, Erington had killed himself in circumstances which suggested he could have been murdered. So further enquiries would have to be made. And sooner or later, Salas would have to be informed . . .

On Wednesday morning there was a sudden change of weather: the sky was cloudy and the wind, which had veered to the north, blew quite strongly. There were brief white caps to small waves in the bay and water-skiers had to keep within the lee of the spit of land on which the eastern lighthouse lay: sailing boats, instead of ghosting along with constantly slackening sails, surged through the creaming water with taut sheets.

Alvarez left the road and drove up the dirt track as far as the Cardells' caseta, where he parked. Cardell was planting seedlings and his wife was irrigating, using a mattock to open up the channels between rows of plants. They both looked up briefly, then resumed working. This was no time for a break and if the matter was important, he would come and speak to them.

He said, when within earshot of Cardell: 'You'll have heard the Englishman at Ca Na Nadana was shot Monday night?'

Cardell nodded as he continued to work with the slow rhythm which he could maintain all day long. He reached the end of one row and started to plant up the next one.

'D'you hear a shot that night?'

'I didn't.' He jerked his head in the direction of his wife, who was fifty metres away. 'She did.'

Alvarez went over to where she was working in bare feet.

He watched her lift out a mattockful of soil to allow the water to run up a channel, then said: 'Simón says you heard a shot Monday night?'

The channel was full of water. She plugged up the entrance with earth, opened up the next one. 'Aye.'

'Not still being kept awake with the toothache, are you?'

She wore a wide-brimmed straw hat to protect her face and neck from the sun and this bobbed up and down as she nodded.

'Why don't you go and see a dentist?'

She ignored the question. The flow of water, coming from the estanque, was very fast and because of his questions she had not concentrated as hard as she should on what she was doing and the channel was now overfull. She hastily plugged it, splashing them both as she did so.

'Any idea what the time was when you heard the shot?'

'Near enough eleven.'

Dr Rosselló had estimated the time of death as about eleven. 'D'you have any idea in which direction the shot came from?'

She jerked her head to the north.

'Was it far away?'

'Can't say. It sounded different.'

'In what kind of way?'

'Just different.'

'Has there been much shooting around here recently?' It was not the shooting season, but no true Mallorquin worried about details like that.

'Not since the heat came.'

'Did you hear any cars or Mobylettes going up the dirt track before the shot?'

'There were one or two.'

'And afterwards?'

'There were one or two.'

Nothing to be gained there. In the middle of summer,

eleven was not late. The men and women who owned the fields, in which there were usually sheds if not small, uninhabited casetas, often worked them and then stayed on for alfresco suppers or even for the sheer pleasure of being on their own land: the English couple might have been returning to their house: courting couples, needing the solitude which only fifteen years ago they would rightly have been denied, were forever seeking quiet corners . . .

He thanked her. She went on working, opening up channels, plugging them, bent as if her limbs had been frozen in that position. He returned to his car, after shouting a goodbye to Cardell, and drove past Ca Na Nadana to Ca'n Bispo. Rockford was in the front garden, doing some rough weeding with one of the local hand chopping hoes.

'I must apologize for troubling you again, señor, but I need to ask more questions.'

'No call for an apology: gives me a chance to pack in this job.' Rockford brought a red and white ploughman's handkerchief from his pocket and mopped the sweat from his forehead and face.

'Perhaps you will not mind if I say, senor, that unless you are very used to the heat, it is not a good thing to work out in it at this time of the day.'

'Couldn't agree more. Trouble is, my wife likes the garden neat and tidy at all times . . . Anyway, let's get out of the sun. Come on inside and we'll splice the mainbrace.'

As soon as they were in the sitting-room, Rockford switched on the fan, set on a low table. 'Grab a seat . . . Now, what will you drink?'

'May I have a small brandy with a lot of ice, please?'

After handing Alvarez a glass, Rockford poured himself a drink and then sat in the second armchair. He raised his own glass. 'As we used to wish our shipmates:

"Hulls of steel and decks of teak, Captains kind and almost meek, Ladies lush and rather weak, Bunks of joy which never creak." '

'Señor, you will understand that I have come here because of the death of Señor Erington?'

'I've guessed that much . . . Some people have been saying he committed suicide. Wouldn't know about that, but if he did, I'm surprised. Never thought he'd got it in him.'

'It first appeared to be suicide, but now there seems to be the possibility it was murder.'

'Good God? What in the hell is this part of the world coming to?'

'That is a question which I ask myself . . . Will you tell me, please, did you hear a shot on Monday night, after it was dark?'

'I didn't, that's for sure. We went to bed pretty early and I'm one of those blokes who puts his head on the pillow and starts snoring. May have told you before. But I think my wife mentioned something about hearing one.'

'Would it be possible to speak to her about it?'

'I don't quite know. Thing is, she's lying down on her bed with a nasty headache: had it for some time now.' He spoke jerkily. 'Got me worried, matter of fact. But she won't have the quack in.'

'I wouldn't wish to disturb her at such a moment . . . But perhaps if I give you the questions I would like answered, she might be able to tell you the answers?'

'Don't see why not, so long as she's not asleep. Wouldn't want to wake her up.' He put his glass down and stood. 'What would you like me to ask her?'

'Can the señora say at what time the shot was that she heard: whether it sounded different from the shots one normally hears around here: and finally did any car or Mobylette drive off very soon afterwards?'

Rockford left the room, walking with the spring of someone in good physical condition. He soon returned, sat, and picked up his pipe which, together with a tobacco pouch, had been lying on the table by the side of the chair. 'As I said, my wife heard a single shot. Didn't think much of it then because there are shots going off all the time.'

'But not many in the dark in the middle of the summer?'

'You'd be surprised what the local "sportsmen" get up to. D'you know, there's a man who lives near here who sits under a tree with a gun and plays a tape-recording of a female thrush's call. Any male thrush which comes hot wing and alights on the tree gets blasted: tell that to any dedicated British shot and he'd go purple in the face. Though as I've always said, any thrush that does get shot must have had a very poor bird's IQ.'

'Señor?'

'Sorry about that: never can remember how difficult it is for a foreigner. Bird's eye view. But that won't mean anything in Spanish . . . Forget it and have another drink?' He stood.

'Perhaps just a small one, thank you, señor. Did the señora notice anything special about the shot?'

Rockford took Alvarez's glass and answered as he went through to the kitchen to pour out the drinks. 'As far as she was concerned, it was just one more shot.' He put his head through the hatchway. 'She didn't notice the time, either, but as she knows she put her light out at twenty past eleven, it must have been a bit earlier than that.'

'Did any vehicle drive away afterwards?'

'She thinks she heard one pass here after the shot, but she can't be certain. You know how it is? If you've no reason for noticing at the time, when you try to think back things often get a bit woolly.'

'Of course.' If the car had passed this house then it almost certainly had nothing to do with the death of Erington. Not that, he thought, there had been any car or Mobylette driving away from Ca Na Nadana just after the shot. The experts had theorized and, typically, had merely succeeded in confusing a very simple fact. Erington had committed suicide.

CHAPTER 23

Because Salas was the kind of man he was—arrogant, small-minded, pernickety, always demanding every i to be dotted twice and every t to be crossed thrice—it was going to be necessary before the case was closed to show that all possible enquiries had been made and these, however unnecessary they obviously were to anyone of even a little common sense, must of necessity include interviews with anyone who might—by an arrogant, small-minded, pernickety person—be deemed to have had the remotest reason for murdering Erington.

Alvarez braked his car to a halt, with the bonnet just short of the chair, set outside the front door, on which Matas sat. As he climbed out, Matas stared at him with resentment. ' 'Morning, old man.'

Matas hawked and spat.

'Did I tell you that the word "Putta" now stands out beautifully on the lawn at Ca Na Nadana?'

'I don't know nothing about that.'

'You're more stubborn than the old mule my father worked just before he died.'

If anything, Matas accepted that as a compliment.

'I want to know something. Where were you on Monday night?'

'In Madrid, in bed with a couple of blondes.'

'No wonder you look peaked. Didn't anyone tell you that Madrid's tiring at this time of the year?'

'No one don't tell me anything.'

'Have a fag and cheer up.'

Matas looked at the pack he was being offered. 'I don't like 'em.'

'Sorry about that. Trouble is, I can't afford the luxury makes. Have to buy all the tomatoes I eat.'

'They was my tomatoes,' Matas said heatedly. 'I planted the seed, watered 'em . . .'

'I'm still interested in knowing where you were Monday night?'

'Where d'you expect? I was here, that's where.'

'All evening?'

'D'you think the mayor asked me out for a drink?'

'Not unless you were willing to pay for the both of you. Were your wife and Rosa here as well?'

'And that boy what's hanging around our Rosa. If the little bugger thinks he's getting his oar in before she's been up to the altar, he's going to be unlucky.'

'When did he leave?'

'When I kicked him out.'

'Which was when?'

'After the film finished on the telly.'

'The one about the Civil War?'

'What do they want to show that kind of film for? Them of us as was in it just want to forget, that's all.'

Steven Kenley looked horrified. He opened his mouth to speak, said nothing, stared up at the heavens as if expecting them to fall.

'You can't be serious,' said Lettie, not quite as certainly as she would have wished.

'Señora,' replied Alvarez, 'in my job I have to be serious in a matter such as this.'

'But everyone knows he committed suicide. He'd murdered Dolly and you'd found him out.'

'There is, unfortunately, evidence which suggests he may not have committed suicide, he may have been killed.'

She nibbled at her lower lip.

When Alvarez had arrived they'd been sitting out in the front garden in two patio chairs. They now stood by these, bewildered and therefore nervous.

'Señor, all I ask is for you to tell me where you were on Monday evening?'

'But that means you're suggesting I could have . . . have killed Mark. I know I didn't like him. I'm old-fashioned. For me, when a man's a gigolo, he's not much of a man. But I wouldn't kill him because of that. I wouldn't kill anyone because of anything.'

'It's a ridiculous accusation,' said Lettie, having sufficiently regained her composure to be ready to do battle on her husband's behalf.

'Señora, I wish to prove that it is ridiculous.'

'But it's so obvious.'

'To me, yes: but unfortunately not to my senior who is a man of much exactness.'

'I was here on Monday night,' said Kenley. 'And we had two friends in to play bridge.'

'I suppose that's good enough?' demanded Lettie.

'Until what time were you playing, señor?'

'Midnight. We always stop then.'

'May I have their names, please, and where they live?' Alvarez wrote on the back of an envelope he found in his right-hand trouser pocket.

The owner of the garage in which Trent worked was sitting in the very small office. He flashed a number of gold teeth as he spoke. 'Has he been up to something?'

'Not as far as I know,' replied Alvarez.

'Then why d'you want to speak to him?'

'To find out how much you're fiddling the law these days.'

The owner of the garage laughed.

'Where is he?'

'Been taking a car to a customer at the Hotel Azul.' He turned to look at the clock on the wall. 'Should have been back here before now.'

'Try paying him a proper wage and see if that'll help him keep better time.'

'What's he been saying?'

'That you're smart.'

'A man's got to be smart to survive.'

'Sometimes one wonders if it's worthwhile.'

Trent walked into the garage. When he saw Alvarez, his expression hardened.

'Come and have a coffee with me?' said Alvarez.

'It's working hours,' objected the owner.

'Then keep working. We're off for a coffee.'

They walked to the nearby café on the main road, and sat. Alvarez ordered coffee. 'How is the señorita?'

'She's all right. But I don't imagine you've brought me here to talk about her,' replied Trent belligerently.

'Very well. You will have heard that Señor Erington has died?'

'Yes.'

'Perhaps you have also heard that he committed suicide? Now, it is possible he did not commit suicide.'

'Yeah?'

'You are not surprised?'

'Why should I be if the clumsy bastard killed himself accidentally?'

'The possibility is that he was murdered.'

Trent stared at him with astonishment.

'So now I have to ask more questions. Will you tell me, please, where you were on Monday evening?'

'Working, like always.'

'And when you had finished at the garage?'

'I went out with Carol.'

'Where did you go?'

Trent hesitated briefly, then said: 'To Cala Tellai: had

a picnic supper and a late swim.'

'How did you go there?'

'In a car.'

'Your own?'

'No.'

'Perhaps you borrowed one from the garage.' There was no answer. Alvarez smiled. 'Señor, I am a detective, but that does not mean I cannot understand that when a man is exploited because he does not have a work permit, from time to time, perhaps unwisely, he gets a little of his own back by keeping a car which has been out on hire and not returning it to the garage until the following day . . . At what time did you return from Cala Tellai?'

'I don't know . . . Around midnight.'

'Was the señorita with you all the time?'

'If you don't believe me, ask her.'

'I probably shall, since it is necessary for my report that I do, but I have no doubts.'

The waiter arrived with the coffee, set the cups and saucers on the table, and filled them.

'What happens next?' demanded Trent, once the waiter had left.

'As far as you are concerned, nothing.' Alvarez opened a packet of sugar and poured the contents into his coffee.

Victoriana's parents lived on the outskirts of Inca, near to the railway station: from the sitting-room, on the fourth floor of the eight-storey building, one had a dramatic view of the mountains.

'Victoriana has always worked very hard,' said her mother, a small, faded woman in whom it was just possible to see the looks which now bloomed so lushly in her daughter. The wary, even frightened, respect with which she had first faced Alvarez had given way to a protective aggression when it seemed to her that her daughter was being suspected of some wrongdoing.

'Mum, all the detective said . . .' began Victoriana.

She interrupted her daughter. 'I didn't like her working there, and that's straight, not with what went on: but the money was good and the man never bothered her. Then when the señora died, I told her she ought to come home: wasn't right to be there, not when he was on his own.'

'Ana was there, wasn't she?' Victoriana said petulantly.

'Not every night of the week and you know that just as well as me.'

'What if she wasn't? What d'you think I am?'

'The same as any other girl who doesn't know half as much as she thinks she does.' She suddenly accepted Alvarez as a friend, rather than a foe. 'They're all too sure of 'emselves, aren't they?'

He nodded. Victoriana looked scornful. He said: 'I need to know where you were last Monday evening, señorita?'

'Where I am every night now: here.'

'Right in this flat,' agreed her mother. 'Said she was going out to the discothèque, but her dad and me said she wasn't. Tried to argue. Told her, straight, when I was a girl I didn't set foot outside our house on my own and what's more, I didn't want to: there was none of this going off with the boys and only the good Lord knowing what is happening — although a mother can have a good guess.'

'You've just got a nasty mind,' said Victoriana sullenly.

'Not without good reason.'

Alvarez spoke quickly, to avoid what was obviously an often repeated argument. 'And you were in all evening?'

'Didn't get the chance to do anything else, did I, with her treating me like I was ten years old.'

Her mother folded her arms across her ample bosom. 'You live in our house, you live as we say.'

'When did you go to bed?' he asked.

'When the film finished.'

'Was that the one about the Civil War?'

'Yeah. I wanted to watch the other channel, but Dad had to see all that stupid fighting.'

Matas had wanted to forget, her father had wanted to remember. Perhaps they had fought on opposite sides: it was still a question one tried not to ask. He stood. 'Thanks for your help.'

'Is that all?' her mother asked, surprised.

He nodded.

The road out of Inca had recently been resurfaced and now a car rode smoothly instead of bounding from ridge to minor pothole. When he got back to Llueso, Alvarez thought, he'd have a word with Vives and see if Erington had made a will since Señora Lund's death. Assuming he hadn't, he'd go ahead and write his final report. Erington had murdered Señora Lund. It had been a very cleverly planned and executed murder and but for that mistake over the sleeping pills might well have succeeded. But he had made that one mistake and when it had become clear that he was about to be arrested, he had committed suicide.

He began to hum. Once he had handed in his report, he could relax. It didn't do a man of his age any good to work too hard.

CHAPTER 24

Alvarez, in his office, spoke to Vives over the phone.

'As far as I know,' said Vives, in answer to a question, 'he made no will.'

'Will you check with Madrid for me to see if he got anyone else to draw one up for him?'

'I suppose I can.'

Alvarez replaced the receiver. It was no sooner down than the phone rang.

'Palma here. We've had a report on the automatic and the case you sent us. Tests show that the cartridge was fired by the automatic and that the bullet recovered from the body was also fired by it.

'The automatic is a nine millimetre Walther: model P thirty-eight: serial number seven zero two six Q. It is remarkable only for the extreme shortness of the barrel, just six and a half centimetres. Such examples are rare and Germany says it was made in either nineteen-thirty-nine or forty for the Gestapo.'

When the call was over, he opened the middle left-hand drawer of the desk and brought out half a dozen sheets of typing paper. He picked up a ballpoint pen. Remember the memorandum Superior Chief Salas had recently had distributed to all members of the CID. Case reports were being drawn up more and more slackly. Good reports came from sharp thinking, slack reports from sloppy thinking . . . He sighed. Ten to one Salas would describe the coming report as a very slack one indeed.

An hour later, he laid the pen down. He'd noted all the salient points of the case in chronological order, detailed the course of his investigations, summarized witness's statements, etc., etc. Now he was ready to start typing . . .

He suddenly started. Typing! Sweet Mary, but he'd clean forgotten to send the suicide letter to Palma, together with comparison typing from each typewriter in Ca Na Nadana, for tests to be made. Not difficult to imagine what Superior Chief Salas would have thought of such crass carelessness!

He looked at his watch. It was true that there was prob-ably just time to go to Ca Na Nadana, but there might be a small hitch and Dolores did become so upset if he were late for a meal. He'd go in the afternoon.

★

It was ten past five when he stepped out of his car, crossed to the front door of Ca Na Nadana, and rang the bell. He heard Lulu begin to yap.

Ana opened the door. 'Good afternoon, señorita. I just need to check up on something else.'

She stepped to one side and he entered. Lulu's rate of yapping increased until he was inside the hall and then, eyes bulging alarmingly, she stared up at him. It finally occurred to her that she might have met him before. She came forward and smelled his shoes, wagged her tail. He bent down and stroked her head. 'Have you any idea how many typewriters there are in this house?' he asked, as he straightened up.

'There's just one,' she answered immediately.

'That's in the study, here?'

She nodded.

'The señor didn't have one?'

'Not that I know of, but naturally I've never been through everything in his room.'

'Then to make certain I'll go up and check. And after that I'll be doing some typing on the machine down here so don't think it's a ghost.'

'I don't believe in ghosts,' she replied, very seriously.

He went upstairs to Erington's room where he opened the shutters before searching the built-in cupboards. There was no typewriter in any of them, nor—though this was obviously extremely unlikely—was there a small portable in either of the bottom drawers of the dressing-table.

He looked down at the suicide note which still lay on the top of the dressing-table. Remembering what kind of a man Salas was, and in view of the evidence which had to be negated, it was perhaps sensible even at this late stage to ask that both envelope and letter be checked for finger-prints to verify that Erington had handled them. He picked up the envelope by its corners, aware that previously he had handled it without thought, and carried it down to the study.

The typewriter, a portable Olympia, was on a small typing table which had two shallow drawers below the working surface. There was headed notepaper in the top one and he wound a sheet of this into the machine. Carefully, he extracted the letter, unfolded it, and laid it by the side of the typewriter. He typed: 'I can't face any more. I killed Dolly because I wanted her money.' As he struck a wrong key, and swore, it again occurred to him that the message was very curt when surely one would have expected a man of Erington's stamp to try to justify the murder, however ridiculous such justification must seem to someone else? He shrugged his shoulders. Who could judge how any man was likely to write just before he blew his brains out? He withdrew the sheet of notepaper, read through the typing, then initialled the page and added the date for reference purposes: everything according to the book. He visually compared the two examples of type — only an expert could say for sure, but he was satisfied the same machine had typed both.

There was one last thing to do before he left — check that there was not a second typewriter in the master bedroom, or any of the other bedrooms. He returned upstairs, went into the master bedroom, automatically closing the door behind himself. Almost immediately there was a scratching and he let Lulu in. She waddled over to the bed and if one had imagination one could see her desperate hope wither as she discovered, by scent, that the bed was still empty and her mistress had not returned. What was her future? In just eleven days her pampered world had been shattered forever. Eleven days ago, Erington had come into this room as Dolly Lund lay drunkenly asleep and murdered her with a pillow. Lulu, not realizing the significance of what was happening, had probably assumed — assuming that dogs could assume — that this was just one more bout of love-making . . .

The question raced through his mind. Then why had she barked?

He tried to dismiss the question. Perhaps she hadn't. Victoriana could easily have made a mistake: being half woken by some other noise — she'd have sampled the champagne — she had heard the bark of one of the dogs chained to the entrance of a field to 'guard' it and in her half waking, half sleeping state had falsely identified it as Lulu's barking. But all the 'guard' dogs were quite big and their barks were deep-toned: Lulu's yap was high-pitched . . .

If one accepted that it had been Lulu who had barked (or yapped), surely one had to go on to accept that it was very unlikely she'd have barked at Erington. So one had to postulate a third person who'd been present at the death of Dolly Lund. This at once made it probable that Erington had been murdered and had not committed suicide: the motive almost certainly being that Erington was in imminent danger of being arrested and if he were he'd tell the truth.

He sat down on the edge of the bed and Lulu came up to him and worried his trousers until he picked her up and put her down on his lap. She settled and he fondled her ears as she looked up, eyes filled with gratitude. He recalled certain facts, noted at the time but dismissed as being of no consequence. Now, examined in the light of the assumption he had just been forced to make, it became obvious that in dismissing them he might have made a bad mistake.

By the side of the bed had been a newly opened bottle of sleeping pills from which nineteen pills had been missing. Had there been five or less missing it would almost certainly have been assumed that she had swallowed these and, because of the quantity of alcohol she had drunk, they had killed her. Had she been awakened sufficiently to be persuaded to swallow up to five—and a drunken person could often be aroused sufficiently to do something even when not aware of what she was doing—the evidence of having taken them would have been found in the analysis of the contents of her stomach. True, if there had been a post mortem, the assumption that the sleeping pills, aggravated by the effect of the alcohol, had killed her would have been shown not to be true: but wouldn't that assumption merely have been replaced by another? That she had rolled on to her face and suffocated, rolling back in the final paroxysm of death when it was too late? So here was a murder which could have been cleverly concealed, yet had been revealed by the most elementary of mistakes . . . Criminals often made mistakes, else they would not be caught, but would Erington, who had so carefully and cleverly manufactured an alibi for himself, have made so ridiculously elementary a mistake as not to find out how many pills could be taken without the antagonistic substance, ITC, working?

Erington had been both clever and cunning, but he had also been very weak. Clever, cunning men could plot murders, but when it came actually to committing them they could discover that they lacked the necessary courage . . .

On the morning of the murder of Dolly Lund, her bedroom had been very tidy: her underclothes folded on a chair, her frock hanging in the cupboard, her jewels in the jewel-box. Yet she was a very untidy woman who always relied on others to clear up the mess she left behind her. Erington must have realized that to tidy up her room, after it was known she had retired to bed so drunk it was probable she'd be even untidier than usual, could be to arouse suspicion . . .

Erington had almost certainly arrived at the house at

two and left half an hour later. Dr Rosselló had put Dolly Lund's death at four, but because the estimated time of death must never be accepted as accurate, it had been assumed that here there had been a mistake of between one and a half and two hours. But suppose that estimate had been reasonably accurate. Then Erington had ridden away at half past two and someone else had pressed the pillow over the sleeping woman's face much later . . .

When Erington had returned from England on the Monday, he had apparently been shocked by the news of Dolly's death. Then, before he had learned what was the cause of death, he had suggested she must have taken some sleeping pills after drinking over-heavily at her party. At the time, because he was already suspect, his shock had been presumed false and his reference to the sleeping pills a clumsy attempt to reinforce the suggestion that death had been accidental. But if he had not known she was dead, then his shock would have been genuine and his remark about the sleeping pills a natural one to make — more especially if he had known that there had been a new bottle of sleeping pills by her bedside. After all, alcohol often had the effect of inducing immediate sleep, but then waking the drinker up later and leaving him or her unable to return to sleep. In her hazy state, what more natural than that she should have taken some pills . . .

The Mobylette had returned down the dirt track at two-thirty. After that, Carolina Cardell, suffering from toothache, had heard no vehicle pass her house . . .

To turn to the murder of Erington, which had to be directly connected with the murder of Dolly Lund. The automatic was a Walther with a very short barrel and it had been produced for the Gestapo in the first part of the war. Erington appeared to have used it to commit suicide, but its rarity made it that much more difficult for him ever to have obtained it . . .

The suicide note, curt yet to the point, had contained not one word of self-justification . . .

He looked down at Lulu. If only you hadn't yapped, he thought with bitter regret.

CHAPTER 25

Alvarez left Ca Na Nadana and walked up the dirt track to Ca'n Bispo. In the late sunlight, the garden was a dusty place of tired plants and harsh shadows. He knocked on the front door.

Rockford opened the door. 'Hullo, there! You're becoming a regular visitor: come on in.'

They entered the sitting-room.

'More questions, I suppose? But there's time for a noggin first. What'll it be?'

'Nothing, thank you, señor.'

'Nothing? But . . .' He stared at Alvarez's face and what he saw there made him square his shoulders. 'I see.' He crossed to the mantelpiece, picked up his pipe and tobacco pouch, stood with his back to the fireplace, legs wide apart, and began slowly and methodically to pack the bowl of the pipe with tobacco.

'Señor, I need to speak to the señora as well as to yourself.'

'Can't do that, I'm afraid. She's still got that beastly head that's been worrying her for days.'

'Nevertheless . . .'

'No,' said Rockford forcefully.

Alvarez crossed to one of the armchairs. He sat, stared at the worn carpet for several seconds, then looked up. 'Señor, it has taken me a long time, but now at last I know who. But I still do not know why.'

'What's it matter?'

'It could be very important.'

Rockford took a box of matches from his pocket and struck one to light his pipe. When the pipe was drawing well he blew the match out and was about to throw it into the fireplace when he suddenly checked himself and looked round for an ashtray. He found one on an occasional table and dropped the spent match on to it.

'Señor, why was the señora killed?'

Rockford returned to the fireplace. He drew on the pipe, causing it to smoke furiously, and made no attempt to answer for nearly half a minute. Then he took the pipe from his mouth and held it in his right hand. 'I don't suppose you'll be able to understand. Matter of fact, I don't think I do myself . . .'

He smoked, then continued speaking. 'You've got to remember that my wife was the daughter of a very successful naval officer, Admiral Sir Hugh Hobson. Another thing, her mother had a private income for her life from a trust. The family lived really well: you could in those days, you know, with plenty of servants to run the big house and no need to worry about the cost of entertaining . . . A person gets used to living well and then it's not easy to change. Wasn't it Tennyson who said something like, " 'Tis better to have loved and lost, than never to have loved at all"? I've never gone along with that. Better never to taste champagne than to taste it and get to like it and then not be able to afford any. Know what I mean?'

He puffed at the pipe again, to find it had gone out. He put it on the mantelpiece and a little ash spilled out. Very carefully, he scooped the ash into the palm of his hand and carried it over to the ashtray. 'I hadn't any sort of a private income: matter of fact, with my background it was quite something to get into the Navy in those days. So when I married Cynthia, things weren't easy for her. Not that she complained, of course.

'Promotion came much more quickly during the war

and I gained my own command. Last ship was a destroyer, beautiful, smart as a tea clipper, and left all the other ships in the flotilla to pitch in her wake. Matter of fact, I managed to buy her bell when she was broken up fifteen years back, but Cynthia doesn't like that sort of thing about the place . . . Didn't make flag rank, though. Thought I might at one time, but there were too many better men and after the war so many ships were scrapped or mothballed . . .

'Neither of us fancied living in England after I'd retired. Been abroad a lot, you know, and got used to decent weather. Another thing, don't understand the young these days, with all their demonstrations and contempt for the law. Not nice when a country ceases to be proud of itself . . .

'Had a bit of a job finding the money to buy this house and still have enough to live on, but we managed. Been very happy here: lovely weather, nice people, time to sit back and realize we're lucky to be alive . . . Then my brother had some trouble with his business and needed money and asked me if I could help. One's got to help family, of course . . .' He became silent.

'Did it save his business, señor?'

'What's that? . . . No. Wasn't enough, I suppose. Anyway, lost the lot. That sort of thing happens and there's nothing to be done about it. Trouble was . . . Trouble was, Cynthia couldn't look at it quite like that.' He spoke reluctantly, hating to be seen to criticize his wife. 'She thought I shouldn't have lent the money to my brother, but when it's family . . . Left us in a nasty financial hole. Inflation's been making things more and more difficult and when this happened we were in considerable trouble. Entirely my fault: never made enough to give us a comfortable old age. Meant we now need to sell this house and move to a flat in the Port or else return to England. Upset Cynthia no end, poor old fruit.'

He went over to the window and stared out at Ca Na
Nadana. 'Don't suppose you ever met Dolly Lund? Not
alive, that is. Too much money. It's a funny thing, but
women can't handle a lot of money: always seems to confuse 'em. Though if I said something like that back home
now, I'd be in trouble: no right of free speech left there.
But it's fact. Dolly was always trying to impress and didn't
care how unsubtle she was. Used to upset Cynthia because
she'd been brought up so differently. And it came even
harder on her, seeing money thrown around while we
were faced with selling this place and moving into a flat
because we'd run out of money . . .

'Went to the party that Saturday. Too much of everything right from the start. And then Dolly, well above the
Plimsoll line in champers, began to boast about how
smart she was in business and how in the past few months
she'd made forty thousand pounds and bought the brooch
she was wearing: chap said it looked like costume
jewellery. Don't hold with being rude myself, but I must
admit I had a quick chuckle over that.'

He turned, walked over to the second armchair and
sat. He was suddenly looking quite old and his face was
very drawn. 'By the time we got back here, Cynthia had
had rather a lot of champagne: in a funny way which I
don't pretend to be able to understand, she'd been showing her contempt by drinking . . .' He became silent. He
looked around for his pipe, remembered it was on the
mantelpiece, relaxed back in the chair. He ran his hand
over his hair. 'She started talking about the party and
what it must have cost and how Dolly had spent forty
thousand on a brooch when she'd already so much
jewellery it was vulgar while we had so little money we
were going to have to move into a flat . . . Cutting a long
story short, we went to bed and, as always, I fell asleep
right away. But I'd had a solid measure of drink, like
everyone else, and it woke me up during the night and it

was a quick trip along the corridor to pump ship. Then I couldn't get back to sleep. In the end, I went for a walk: only thing to do. Halfway along to Ca Na Nadana and one of those midget motorized bikes came up from the road and turned into the drive and I thought I recognized the rider. But according to Dolly, who'd been furious about it, Mark was in England because his mother was ill. I started wondering if something funny was up so I went to the house. The front door wasn't locked. Shouldn't have gone inside, of course: wouldn't have done but for all that champagne. Everything was a bit blurred . . .'

Alvarez finally interrupted him. 'Senor, I know that it was not you who went into Ca Na Nadana, it was your wife.'

'No!'

He said sadly: 'Would you ever have bothered to tidy the clothes which had been thrown on the floor? Did it matter at all to you if the senora had spent forty thousand pounds on a brooch?'

'I swear it wasn't Cynthia.'

'When I came here I knew it was your wife who had killed Señora Dolly Lund. What I did not know was why. Now, I think I begin to understand.'

Rockford clenched his fists so tightly that the knuckles whitened: his face worked as if he were in pain. 'Then you're a damn sight cleverer than I am. I . . . I don't begin to understand though I've tried and tried.'

'Señor, it is necessary to remember that to a man a home is something less than it is to a woman. For him, it is where he returns after work, has a drink, eats the meals his wife has prepared for him, goes to bed. It is this also for a woman, but then it is something more. She sees it as the shield which protects her family, it is where she has given herself to her man in love, it is memories . . . Take away her home and you destroy so much.'

'We'll be able to afford a small flat in the Port: at the

back, away from the sea,' he said, in a strained voice.

'But the change will be made because it is forced on you, not because you wish it.'

'She wouldn't look at things calmly. What was the point of blaming Dolly? Nothing would have changed for us if Dolly had given the whole forty thousand to charity instead of spending it on that brooch.'

'Of course not, señor, but how is a woman faced with the loss of her home to think with cold logic? She thinks with her heart. She sees a huge sum of money wasted, when just a small proportion of it could save her home. So she sees this other woman, living in a luxurious home which no one can take from her, even keeping a paid man to serve her when she wishes, as mocking her in her tragedy.'

Rockford said wonderingly: 'God knows, I'm married to her but you seem to understand her better than I do.'

'You are too close to her to be able to understand.'

He shook his head. He was not denying the probability: he was again admitting his complete bewilderment.

'It was your wife who woke early Sunday morning, wasn't it, señor?'

He nodded. 'Said I was snoring louder than the old *Queen Mary*'s foghorn . . . Couldn't get back to sleep with such a racket so she got up and made herself some tea and drank it in this room. Saw a motorized bike come along the dirt track and stop at the gates of Ca Na Nadana. The rider didn't cut the engine so the headlight remained on. Cynthia wondered what was happening and picked up our pair of binoculars and looked through 'em. She recognized Mark Erington, even though he was supposed to be back in England. After a bit, the bike went into the drive and out of sight of here.

'She went to see what was happening . . .' He stopped, was silent for a long while, then said: 'She was too upset to think straight—things always seem far worse in the middle of the night, don't they? But to tell the truth I've wondered if, in her confusion, and in an odd way, she was hoping to find out something that in her mind would mean she'd get her own back on Dolly: but maybe that's twisting everything into knots. She was wearing a house-coat over her nightdress and she just went straight out of the house like that . . . I mean, normally she'd never have done such a thing . . .

'When she got to the drive she found the bike was there, but there was no sign of Erington. She waited quite a while, then walked up to the front door which was open. That's when Erington came hurrying out of the place. Came face to face with her and shouted with fear. No guts in the man. So frightened, he began to babble about what he'd been going to do, but hadn't been able to. She didn't understand the half of what he told her. Then he swore he'd help her all he could if she never told anyone she'd seen him, got back on to the bike, and rode off. Cynthia was certain she was in a nightmare. Erington was in England but he'd just come running out of the house, she was standing in her nightdress and housecoat in front of Ca Na Nadana when she ought to be in bed, and something he'd said, which she couldn't remember, ter-rified her . . . But she couldn't find any way of escape.

'You know how it is sometimes, when you're scared of doing something but you seem unable to prevent yourself doing it? It was like that with her. She knew there was something horrible inside the house and yet she couldn't stop herself going inside. She switched lights on in several of the downstairs rooms. She stared at all the valuable furniture, hating Dolly more and more for owning it . . . It was all so crazy. I've asked her time and time again why she did all that and all she can answer is, it was the nightmare . . .

'In the end, she went up to Dolly's bedroom. Even switched on the light there, which shows she'd no real idea of what she was doing. The jewellery was scattered around the top of the dressing-table and she picked up the brooch. Kept thinking, forty thousand pounds.'

'Ah!' said Alvarez suddenly.

'What's that?'

'I believe I now know about those two scratches on the inside of one of the windows. Has your wife said what she did with the brooch?'

'Put it in the jewel-box where it ought to have been.'

'But before that?'

'As far as I know, she didn't do anything.'

'Nevertheless, I think she tried the diamond on the glass to see if it scratched it because that's popularly supposed to be the test of a real diamond and she was hoping it would fail . . . What happened next, señor?'

'She doesn't know,' he answered, in a voice now so low it was little above a whisper. 'She can't remember a thing.'

'Have you tried to help her discover just a little of what took place?'

'No.'

'Because you are frightened to?'

'No,' he replied, his voice now forceful.

'Then you have no fear that possibly she was aware of just a little of what she was doing?'

'She couldn't have known or she wouldn't have done it.'

'Señor, you are a man of very great strength when it comes to those you love. Here you know there are questions which should be answered, yet you will never ask them because once the answers have been given they can never be recalled.'

'I don't know what the devil you're talking about.'

Those sleeping pills, he thought. Taken from the bottle to make death seem accidental, as Erington had planned. Yet why should she have sought to do that unless she knew there was a need to do so if she were to protect herself?

And if she could clearly see this, then her mind could not have been so confused . . .

'She was in a nightmare. She couldn't possibly have meant to kill Dolly.'

Alvarez studied him and saw mental agony and desperation: he saw a man who feared and yet would not admit, even to himself, that he feared.

Rockford suddenly stood. He went over to the fireplace, picked up the pipe, and struck a match.

'Senor, did you during the war obtain a Walther automatic with a very short barrel?'

The match had burned down. Rockford extinguished it by rapidly waving his hand in the air. He looked at the charred stub, then with careful deliberation he threw it into the clean fireplace. 'We brought a couple of army officers home on my ship and one of 'em gave it to me. Said he took it off a gestapo type he'd been interrogating in connection with some particularly nasty killings.'

'And you used it to shoot Erington?'

'Yes.'

'Why did you shoot him?'

'That's obvious enough, isn't it?' He spoke briskly now that everything was easily understandable. He leaned sideways and tapped the pipe against the side of the fireplace: ash fell on to the bricks.

'He told you that since he had not killed the señora, he knew that your wife must have done?'

'In a hell of a panic, he was.'

'And if I arrested him, he was going to tell me the full truth?'

'No guts.'

'So you killed him to keep him quiet?'

'I killed him to try and prevent anything happening to Cynthia.' He tamped down the tobacco which remained in the bowl of the pipe. Then he struck another match and drew the flame into the pipe. Once it was going well, he flicked the match into the fireplace. 'All right, what happens now? I need to tell Cynthia. Going to be difficult. Poor old thing's in a terrible state. Won't see the doctor, hard as I've tried to persuade her to.'

'Señor, it seems certain that the real Samantha Waite, daughter of Dolly Lund, must be in serious financial trouble — there remains a little of the copy of a letter her mother wrote to her and from this it is clear that she asked for help which her mother refused. If it becomes certain that Erington did not murder Señora Lund, then his estate will probably inherit all her wealth — a foreigner in Spain can leave her property how she wishes and does not have to observe Spanish law which says a proportion must be left to her children. Since he intended to murder her but lacked the courage to do so, it would be morally very wrong that his estate should so benefit. On the other hand, if it is held that he did murder the señora, then because a man may not benefit from his own crime, his estate will receive nothing under the will. In this case, Señora Lund will be held to have died intestate and eventually, since the law for foreigners moves just as slowly as it does for Spaniards, her estate, less taxes, will pass to her daughter. Morally, this would be very right . . . I do not think it should be difficult for the English police to discover where the real Señora Waite is now living.'

'What are you saying?'

'I find it difficult to express myself clearly, because I am not good at complicated thoughts. But what I am trying to say is that there are times when the law by demanding that the guilty be punished makes it inevitable that the innocent be made to suffer: that for justice to be done, injustice must also be done. I am trying to express my belief that the same act can under one set of circumstances deserve condign punishment and under another set of circumstances call only for deep compassion.

'Señor, there are certain facts in this case which I have not yet presented to my superiors because until today I have not considered such facts of any importance. Unless they are now presented it will inevitably be agreed, even by my superior chief, that Erington murdered the señora and afterwards committed suicide because he was terrified of being arrested and charged with murder.

'Only three people will know the truth. You, your wife, and me. I will not be troubled by the knowledge, for reasons I have tried to give. How you and your wife learn to live with the truth is a problem I am sure you will solve because you are a man of much courage. Perhaps—and I do not wish to be impertinent when I say this—you will find your life more sympathetic: your wife will need much love and it is difficult to receive without giving, even if just a little.'

Dolores looked across the supper table at Alvarez. 'Enrique, what's the matter?'

'Nothing.'

'But you've hardly spoken all evening.'

'He's not a woman,' said Jaime scornfully.

'Who asked you to speak like a fool?'

'I may speak like a fool, but at least I know what's worrying him. He's got an empty glass.'

'All the better for it,' she replied sharply.

Jaime pushed the bottle of red wine across the table.

Alvarez filled his glass. 'There's nothing wrong with me: it's just that I've been wondering.'

'About women?'

'About an Englishman I've met.' He drank. 'I've been wondering if he's been thinking that justice may occasionally be done, but it must never be seen to be done.'

They stared blankly at him.

'It's a play on the word "done" . . . Forget it.'

They forgot it.